THE MYSTERY OF THE
PHANTOM GRASSHOPPER

Your TRIXIE BELDEN Library

Trixie Belden and the
MYSTERY OF THE PHANTOM GRASSHOPPER

BY KATHRYN KENNY

Cover by Jack Wacker

GOLDEN PRESS
Western Publishing Company, Inc.
Racine, Wisconsin

CONTENTS

THE MYSTERY OF THE PHANTOM GRASSHOPPER

Downtown • 1

THE BIG STATION WAGON with the legend BOB-WHITES
OF THE GLEN lettered on one door headed into Sleepyside and pulled into the parking lot alongside the
common.

Trixie Belden opened a rear door and stepped out.
"Last one in, first one out," she said. "You boys can
close the windows and lock the car. Honey and Di
and I are going ahead to say hello to Hoppy."

13

Mart Belden, often mistaken for Trixie's twin, shook his head. "Come on, Trixie," he yelped. "Ever since Moms told you about talking to that old weather vane on top of Town Hall, you've gone bananas. Aren't you ever going to give it up?"

"Never!" Trixie declared. "Moms still does it once in a while." She chuckled. "Now I've got Honey and Di doing it!"

Di Lynch's big violet eyes sparkled in response. "We're going to say hello to Hoppy until we're old, old ladies," she said.

Dan Mangan looked bewildered. He hadn't lived in Sleepyside for very long and wasn't sure what Trixie was talking about. "What's this all about?" he asked.

Jim, Honey's adopted brother, and Brian, Trixie's other brother, shrugged good-naturedly. Both boys were seventeen and amused by Trixie's occasionally superstitious ways.

"It's a family thing, Dan," Brian explained. "When Moms was a little girl, she and her mother always used to say hello to the weather vane when they passed the common. My grandmother said that it brought good luck."

"When Moms told Trixie," Mart added, "Trixie

14

wanted me and Brian to start doing it, too. Trouble is, people think you're pixilated when they hear you talking to a weather vane."

Honey Wheeler made a face. "I don't know what that means," she said. "But Di and I agree with Trixie—it's a nice tradition to say hello to Hoppy."

As the girls started off, Dan called, "Yeah, but does it work? Have you had any good luck lately?"

Laughing, Trixie called back, "Not yet. But Hoppy will make us famous someday. We'll meet you over by Town Hall."

Jim waved them on. "We'll be right there," he said. "We don't want to be late for the movie."

"And we need plenty of time to eat at Wimpy's first," Mart added. "I'm positively bulimic!"

While the girls crossed the common, Jim locked up the station wagon. Honey's wealthy father had given the station wagon to the young people after buying a new car for himself. Each of them owned one seventh of the car, and they were almost as proud of it as they were of their club.

The Bob-Whites of the Glen was not merely a fun club. One of the reasons the club was formed was to help people who needed help. The seven club members were always busy with some special project—

raising funds for UNICEF or donations for earthquake victims, or working for the Heart Fund.

Somehow, along the way, Trixie always managed to get them involved in a mystery. Lively and inquisitive, Trixie was attracted to mysteries like a magnet. She seemed to have a special knack for solving cases that baffled police and detectives. Once, Trixie had helped capture a gang of sheep rustlers out in Iowa. Another time, she'd led the FBI to a spy ring operating on the Mississippi River. It was no wonder that she dreamed of the day when she and Honey, her best friend, would form the Belden-Wheeler Detective Agency.

Honey and Jim lived at Manor House, a beautiful large estate on the hill above the Beldens' Crabapple Farm.

Honey had been delicate and shy when she moved to Sleepyside-on-the-Hudson, but now she was healthy and outgoing. Trixie's clever detective work had helped to prove that Jim was heir to a fortune of his own. Someday, Jim hoped to use his inheritance to open a school for homeless boys. Jim had been homeless himself until the Wheelers had adopted him, and he knew how badly such boys needed help and guidance.

Jim had taught his friends the Bob-White whistle that was the club's secret signal and had inspired the club's name. He and Trixie were copresidents. Vice-president Honey, who loved to sew, had designed and made the red jackets worn by each of the club members.

Brian was a charter member of the club. Serious and quiet, he planned to become a doctor and work with Jim at his home for boys. Mart was the secretary-treasurer. He enjoyed confusing the others by using big words.

Diana Lynch and Dan Mangan were also members of the club. Di came from a wealthy family, like Honey, and lived in a great stone mansion farther down the road from Crabapple Farm. Di was the prettiest girl in school, with long black hair and big violet eyes. But she, too, had been lonely and unhappy until Trixie and the others had made her their friend.

Dan Mangan, the seventh club member, was the nephew of Bill Regan, the man in charge of the Wheelers' stable of riding horses. Dan had been a city tough, in trouble with the police, until Regan had brought him to Sleepyside. Now he lived with Mr. Maypenny, the Wheelers' elderly gamekeeper, and helped care for the wild game preserve. The friendship of the Bob-Whites had encouraged Dan to change his tough ways.

Together, the seven club members had shared many exciting adventures.

Scuffing their feet through the red and yellow leaves that covered the common, Trixie, Honey, and Di headed for the Town Hall. The old-fashioned town square always seemed to look prettiest when it was shaded in twilight shadows. The library was dark and deserted, but the lights were turned on in the police station. Even in the fading light, the old Town Hall presented an impressive silhouette against the stately elms behind it.

Tall and narrow, the two-story white clapboard building was one of the oldest landmarks in Sleepyside. Three wooden steps led to the heavy front door. There were many tall, small-paned windows, and a slanted roof that rose sharply, coming to a high peak where a cupola was set. The bell that had once hung in the old bell tower had been gone for many years, but the original weather vane, shaped like a grasshopper, was still perched atop the cupola.

Standing well back from the building, Trixie,

Honey, and Di looked up at the old grasshopper. "Hello, Hoppy," they called softly.

Trixie flipped her fingertips in a small wave.

"That old copper grasshopper really is a handsome weather vane," Honey said.

"He sure is," Trixie agreed.

Mart came rustling through the leaves. "You guys can talk to weather vanes if you like," he said. "I'll stick to ambulating through the fallen leaves until I'm an old man."

Behind him, Dan, Jim, and Brian laughed. "At fifteen," Jim said, "you have a long way to go. Right now, we'd better head for the diner, or we'll never make it to the early show."

Minutes later, the Bob-Whites were crowded into one booth beside the window, joking and teasing while they made a meal of juicy double hamburgers and crisp French fries.

Trixie tapped on the window and waved to someone passing outside. The young woman looked up quickly and, seeing Trixie, smiled and waved before hurrying along.

"Miss Lawler," Trixie informed the others, gesturing with an oversized pickle. "I'll bet she's going to the movie, too. I like her—she's nice."

19

Miss Lawler was a new teacher's aide at Sleepyside Junior-Senior High School. She assisted Miss Craven in social studies classes. All of the Bob-Whites were in Miss Craven's classes at various times during the day, and they all enjoyed it. Trixie and Honey were together in the same class during the last period of the day.

"Poor Miss Lawler," Honey said softly. "She seems so shy. She's always alone." For just a moment, a shadow of sadness appeared in Honey's eyes as she remembered her own days of loneliness, before she met Trixie and the other Bob-Whites.

"I've noticed that, too," Di said. "She's very nice, and I think she's pretty. But she doesn't seem to have any friends."

"Listen," Brian said, "she's only been in town for a couple of weeks—just since school opened. Give her time to get acquainted."

Trixie looked thoughtful. "I wonder where she comes from," she said.

Honey nodded. "So do I. Miss Lawler seems like too good a teacher to be just an aide."

"She really can make things interesting," Trixie said. "She's been showing the class some of the old coins from Mr. Quinn's collection and explaining how much you can learn about history from coins. It's really neat!"

"Yeah," Mart said, putting more salt on his French fries, "she's quite a numismatist."

Trixie raised her eyebrows. "A new-miss-*what*-ist?" she asked.

"A numismatist," Mart repeated. "That's somebody who knows a lot about coins, dear sister."

Trixie grinned. "Well, that's Miss Lawler," she said. "I'm sure glad that Dad talked Mr. Quinn into lending his coin collection to the school. Those old coins really are interesting."

"Some of them are pretty valuable, too," Brian reminded her. "But I guess someone as rich as Mr. Quinn can afford a hobby like that."

Di flipped her long black hair back and looked at her wristwatch. "It's almost time for the show to begin," she admonished.

"Hey, you're right," Dan said. "Let's get going."

Paying their bill quickly, the young people hurried across the street to the theater.

Two hours later, the Bob-Whites were walking back to the parking lot, cutting across the common. It was a beautiful October night. Only a few stars were out, but a round orange moon hung low in the sky.

"A pumpkin moon," Trixie said.

Di sighed wistfully. "It's kind of romantic-looking," she said. "It makes me wish the movie had been a love story."

"Humph," Dan humphed. "Give me a giant gorilla anytime!" He hunched his shoulders and scuffed through a thick pile of leaves, imitating a gorilla.

Mart pounded his chest and growled. "Want to see me climb up the side of the Town Hall?" he asked in a deep, rumbling voice.

The others laughed and threw handfuls of leaves at Dan and Mart.

"Hoppy would kick you right off the roof," Trixie gibed, looking up at the old weather vane.

Brian noticed Miss Lawler passing the common and motioned the others to stop throwing leaves.

"Hi, Miss Lawler," Trixie called. "Did you enjoy the movie?"

The teacher's aide waved and stopped for a moment. "Yes, I did," she answered.

"So did we," Trixie said. "Say, have you met Hoppy?"

Miss Lawler walked across the square to join the

young people. "No, I don't believe I have," she said doubtfully, looking from one young person to the next.

"Well," Trixie told her, "you simply have to meet him right now. Hoppy's the copper grasshopper up there on top of Town Hall. See him? He's over two hundred years old, and he's been standing in that very spot practically since Sleepyside was settled."

"Why, how interesting!" Miss Lawler exclaimed. "He's a real antique!" She stepped back a few steps and craned her neck to get a better look at the ancient weather vane.

With an impish grin, Trixie turned her back on the boys. "If you want some good luck, Miss Lawler, all you have to do is—" Trixie stopped and frowned as a strange *chop-chop-chop* sound, growing louder by the minute, drowned out her voice.

"What's making that awful noise?" Honey shouted.

Brian pointed to a light in the sky, moving steadily closer as the noise grew louder. "A helicopter," he yelled over the loud *chop-chop-chop*.

As they all watched, the helicopter swung low and circled the small common, hovering briefly over the Town Hall. Then it rose swiftly and darted out of sight behind some trees.

"Wonder who that was," Mart said as the noise faded.

"It might have been Mr. Perkins, the radio station manager," Brian said. "Sometimes he has a helicopter shuttle service fly him to the city and back."

Dan rubbed his ears. "Boy, for a minute I thought they were going to land right here on the common," he complained.

"Welome to the new, ultra-modern Sleepyside International Airport," Mart announced in his tour guide voice, gesturing dramatically at the tree-lined common.

Miss Lawler joined in the laughter that followed the announcement. "Trixie," she said, "you started to tell me something about good luck. I'd like to hear about it."

Trixie grinned, feeling a little silly. "Well, we think it's good luck to say hello to Hoppy when you pass by," she said. "At least, Honey and Di and I do. The boys think we're foolish."

"Good luck?" Miss Lawler seemed to think this over. Then she smiled. "Well, I could certainly use some of that," she said. And with a wave of her hand, she called, "Good evening, Hoppy!"

"Miss Lawler," Trixie said impulsively, "you must

24

get lonesome on Sundays. Why don't you come out to Crabapple Farm tomorrow? That's our home—it's only about two miles out of town. My parents love to have visitors. Please drive out and see us."

The teacher's aide shook her head. "I—I don't drive, Trixie," she said. "I'm afraid I can't accept your kind invitation."

"Could we drive you home now?" Honey asked quickly. "We have our station wagon—"

"No, thank you," Miss Lawler said quickly. "I'll see you all in school on Monday. Good night." Turning abruptly, she hurried away without looking back at the Bob-Whites.

During the ride home, Trixie sat in the front seat beside Jim. While the others discussed the movie, Trixie tuned in WSTH, the local radio station that belonged to Mr. Perkins. The station was the favorite of everyone in town because of the wide variety of music played. Mr. Perkins had a large collection of old jazz and swing recordings that the adults loved —Glenn Miller, Benny Goodman, the Dorsey brothers, George Gershwin, and many others. His son Jeff, who was away at college, saw to it that the station also had all the current rock and popular hits that the young people enjoyed. Various times of the day

25

were devoted to one type of music or the other, and requests from listeners for specific songs were always welcome.

"Hey, why so quiet, Trix?" Mart asked after a while. "What ponderous ruminations are you cogitating about now?"

"I'm *thinking* about Miss Lawler," Trixie answered. "She didn't act very shy when I introduced her to Hoppy. But when I invited her to visit Crabapple Farm, she seemed—almost afraid. I think there's something kind of—"

"—strange about Miss Lawler," the other Bob-Whites chorused. They all burst out laughing.

"You're always saying that about somebody, Trixie," Jim said.

"Well, it's true," Trixie insisted, though she couldn't help giggling herself.

"Trixie," Di said when everyone had finished laughing, "did you know the button is missing from your right jacket cuff?"

"I know," Trixie confessed, embarrassed. "It popped off the other day, and you know how I hate to sew. . . ."

"Ah-*ha!*" Mart pointed an accusing finger. "Remember the club rule about keeping our jackets neat and clean? Untidy habiliments are a bad reflection on the Bob-Whites. As secretary-treasurer, I hereby impose a fine of ten cents a day until the button is replaced."

"Oh, Mart," Trixie wailed, "I can't even *find* the button. I'll sew it on as soon as I find it, okay?"

"Ten cents a day," Mart repeated.

Chuckling, Jim swung the car slowly into the driveway at Crabapple Farm. "Better find that button and sew it on, fast," he said.

"I'll have to," Trixie moaned. "Jeepers! I can't afford ten cents a day for very long." She and her brothers climbed out of the station wagon.

Honey rolled down her window. "Don't forget that we have to exercise the horses tomorrow. We'll see you at the stable right after lunch."

Di yawned. "I'm glad that doesn't include me," she said sleepily. "I won't see any of you tomorrow. We'll have company from out of town."

Trixie watched the station wagon back down the driveway and scratched her head. "If Miss Lawler doesn't drive," she muttered, "how does she get around?"

"You don't drive, either," Brian pointed out. "But you get around pretty well."

"I guess you're right," Trixie admitted. "But I wonder why someone as smart as Miss Lawler doesn't know how to drive."

Brian thought for a moment. "It is kind of—"

"Strange," Trixie finished for him. "See what I mean?"

Surprises on Sunday · 2

HALFWAY UP the long hill to Manor House, Trixie started to run. "Let's hurry," she urged her brothers. "We don't want to keep Regan waiting."

Mart looked up the hill, then glanced at his watch. "According to my calculations, I predict we will cover the distance between our present locus and the Wheeler stable, our terminus, in less than one minute," he said calmly. "But just to please you, Trixie, I shall change my *modus operandi* and perambulate at a more expeditious rate."

"Thank you, I think," Trixie said, running on ahead of her brothers.

When the three Beldens reached the stable, Honey, Jim, and Dan were already waiting for them beside the door.

"Hi!" Honey said. "Regan has the horses all ready. Let's go."

Regan was waiting for them inside the cool stable. "Too bad you all have to go to school," he said with a grin. "Now the horses only get ridden on weekends. Any chance of one of you flunking out?"

"No chance!" the young people insisted.

Chuckling to himself, Regan crossed the stable to the row of six stalls. Printed above five of the stalls were the names of the Wheelers' horses: Jupiter, Lady, Susie, Starlight, and Strawberry. Behind their stall doors, the horses stood saddled and waiting. Jupiter, Mr. Wheeler's spirited black gelding, was pawing the ground, impatient and restless.

There was no name above the sixth stall. The young people were surprised to see Regan stop at the door of the stall.

"What's up?" Trixie whispered to Honey.

"I don't know," Honey said, as puzzled and surprised as Trixie.

30

Regan's green eyes twinkled brightly. With a great flourish, he threw open the door to the sixth stall.

A small Shetland pony stood there, looking out at them with soft, doleful eyes. A little boy dressed in a scarlet riding coat was standing beside the pony, holding the reins.

"Bobby!" Trixie exclaimed.

Her six-year-old brother straightened his jacket and led the pony out to the middle of the floor. In a serious tone, he said, "Trixie . . . everybody . . . meet Mr. Pony." Then he smiled. "It was a secret, and I never told *anybody*—'cept Moms and Dad," he crowed.

Regan grinned. "I've been training this pony for a friend of your father's, Honey," he said. "And I needed a small rider to help me. So I taught Bobby to ride."

Bobby nodded vigorously. "Wait till you see how good he taught me to ride!" he shouted. Impatient to show off, he wiggled out of his riding coat and handed it to Trixie. "Help me up, please, Regan," he said.

Outside in the big pasture, Bobby rode Mr. Pony around and around. He sat straight and tall in the saddle and held the reins with a firm hand. The

Bob-Whites leaned against the fence to watch.

"Look at him," Brian whispered. "Bobby rides like a pro."

Honey was impressed. "He's a natural," she said in agreement.

"Well . . ." Trixie said with a shrug, "I guess he gets his talent from me."

Mart reached over and patted Trixie's head. "My sister, the modest one," he said. "Not an ostentatious ossicle in her whole body."

"Oh, go chew on a dictionary," Trixie retorted with a good-natured snicker.

"Okay, you kids," Regan called. "Time for the rest of you to go to work."

He led the horses out from the stable. Bobby sat and watched the Bob-Whites mount their horses and get ready to ride. Trixie could tell by the expression on Bobby's face that he wanted to ride with the "big kids."

Trixie didn't want to hold the others up. "You go ahead," she told them. "I'm going to walk Susie down into the woods so Bobby and I can go riding together."

While riding through the woods, with Bobby beside her on Mr. Pony, Trixie decided that the Wheeler preserve was at its best in October. The sweet scent of pine filled the air, and the bright-colored leaves of the maples and chestnuts growing among the evergreens rustled in the breeze. Trixie watched carefully for rabbits or raccoon but spotted only bushy-tailed gray squirrels scampering about in search of nuts and berries.

"Trixie," Bobby said, "it was nice of you to ride with me."

Trixie brushed aside his thanks. "I wanted to," she told him. "You ride very well."

Bobby grew silent. From the way he was frowning, Trixie knew that he must be thinking something over.

"I have another secret, Trixie," Bobby said. "And I'm going to tell you."

Trixie reined Susie to a stop. "Remember," she cautioned, "a secret isn't a secret anymore if you tell it."

"I know," Bobby said. He took a deep breath. "I have a tree house," he blurted.

Trixie's eyes widened. "A real tree house?" she asked. "Up in a tree?"

Bobby nodded. "Yup," he said. "Regan found the tree, deep in the woods, and we built the house. Want to see it, Trixie?"

An uneasy feeling swept over Trixie. Only a short

distance from the Wheeler preserve, the woods grew very dense and then ended at the edge of a high cliff. All the young people were forbidden to ride near there.

"Wait a minute, Bobby," Trixie said slowly, not wanting to spoil his fun. "Moms won't allow any of us to go deep into the woods. You know that. Regan must have forgotten."

Bobby slid down from Mr. Pony's back and looped the reins over a bush. "We're deep in the woods right now, Trixie," he told her. "Regan said this spot is the deepest part in the whole woods when you ride down through Mr. Wheeler's preserve."

Trixie smiled with relief. "Regan's right," she agreed, dismounting. "We *are* deep in the woods. You can't even tell there's a road over there on the left, behind those trees. We could walk to that road and be out of the deep woods in a minute, if we wanted to."

"But we don't, we don't!" Bobby exclaimed, jumping up and down with excitement. "I'm going to show you my tree house."

"Okay," Trixie said. "Where is it?"

Bobby doubled over with giggles. "Look up above your head, Trixie," he said. "You're leaning against the tree where we built it!"

"Here?" Trixie asked incredulously. Stepping away from the tree, she looked up into the branches. The tree house was nestled in the wide middle section, almost hidden from view. Regan had designed the tree house so expertly that it looked as if it had grown there.

The tree itself was sturdy and not too tall, with strong, low-hanging branches. It was a perfect tree for a small boy to climb in without much danger of falling.

"It's beautiful, Bobby!" Trixie said. "What made you decide to build a tree house?"

"Well," Bobby said, putting his hands in his pockets, "I *had* to. Moms was mad at me 'cause my room was a mess. She says I collect too much junk, but, Trixie, it's *not* junk! My collections are full of real valuable stuff!"

Trixie smiled. "I know, I know," she assured him hastily.

"Come on, I'll show them to you," Bobby urged. He scrambled up into the tree.

Seconds later, Trixie stepped gingerly onto the platform floor of Bobby's tree house. She pivoted slowly on one foot, looking around her. Many of the leaves had fallen from the nearby trees, and Trixie was surprised to see that the old dead-end road was

35

even closer than she had thought. Very few people used the road, and the weather-beaten ROAD ENDS sign looked ready to fall apart.

"Look, here are my collections," Bobby said, pointing to his treasures lined up on the floor. There was a coffee can filled with bottle caps, a mound of "lucky" stones, a lopsided ball of string, a bag full of baseball cards, and a tin can full of buttons. Regan had built a covering over the collections to protect them from the elements.

"I was going to collect bugs, too," Bobby told Trixie, "but Moms says I can't. She says bugs are good for the ground, so I have to leave them there."

"Don't collect snakes, either," Trixie warned. "Are you going to keep all your collections here?" she asked.

Bobby thought that over carefully before answering. "Not everything. If I find something funny, I'll bring it home to show Moms. She can tell me what it is."

Trixie frowned. "Do you mean 'funny ha-ha' or 'funny peculiar'?" she asked.

"What's pick—pickooler mean?" Bobby wanted to know.

"Oh, strange things . . . things you never saw before," Trixie told him.

Bobby nodded. "Yup. The funny things like that I'll bring home to Moms," he said.

The sudden squeal of tires nearby made Bobby jump. "Hey," he shouted, "there's a car out on that road!"

Trixie had only a glimpse of the car as she jumped to her feet. Her ears caught the whinny of a frightened pony.

"Bobby," she cried, "that loud noise scared Mr. Pony! He's running away!" She hurriedly climbed down from the tree.

Susie was tossing her head fretfully and stomping her feet. Off to the left, Trixie could see Mr. Pony thrashing through the bushes.

Swinging into the saddle, Trixie patted Susie, calming her. "It's all right, Susie," she whispered soothingly. "You and I have to catch poor Mr. Pony before he hurts himself."

Bobby reached the ground with tears streaming down his face. "Come back, Mr. Pony," he wailed. "Please don't run away!"

The little pony didn't get far. Trixie spotted him cowering in a clump of heavy bushes, trembling. His coat was dusty and full of burs.

"It's okay, Mr. Pony. Don't be afraid," Trixie said. Gently, softly, she talked to him and tried to calm his

37

fears. She didn't try to touch him until he had stopped shaking. Then, taking his reins, she led the Shetland pony out of the thicket and back to the tree house.

Bobby threw his arms around Mr. Pony's shaggy neck. "Thank you, Trixie," he said, wiping away his tears.

"We'd better go back now, Bobby," Trixie said. "Everybody will be waiting for us."

Honey and the boys were inside the stable, grooming their horses, when Trixie and Bobby got back. Dan had already left to go back to Mr. Maypenny's cottage.

One look at Bobby's tear-stained face and the burs caught in Mr. Pony's shaggy coat, and Regan knew something had gone wrong. Wisely, he asked Bobby no questions about it. "Hi there, fella," he said, lifting Bobby down from the saddle. "Run down to the pasture and get my jacket for me, will you? I left it hanging on the fence."

"Sure," Bobby said. He waved to the "big kids" and ran off on his errand.

"What happened, Trixie?" Regan asked quickly.

Trixie told him about the noisy car. Honey and the boys came out of the stable to listen.

"I didn't know anyone used that old road," Honey said, surprised. "It's a dead end."

Regan's concern had turned to anger. "Those crazy kids," he grumbled. "This summer they were using the road for drag racing. I chased them off half a dozen times, but they came right back. Finally, I told them I'd call the police if I ever saw them back there again. I thought that would keep those young punks away.

"But," Regan continued, "a couple of times while I was building Bobby's tree house, I saw cars drive down the road." He frowned. "I wonder if those kids removed the 'Dead End' sign at the entrance to the road."

"Could be," Trixie said. "We never go into the woods that way, so I don't know. The 'Road Ends' sign is still there; I did see that."

"Well," Regan decided, "I'm going to have to go check on that other sign."

Bobby came dashing back, shouting, "Here's your jacket, Regan!"

"Thanks, fella." Regan grinned. "You and Trixie can go home now. I'll take care of Susie and Mr. Pony."

"Thanks, Regan," Trixie said. Turning to Honey in a sudden brainstorm, she asked, "Why don't you and

Jim come home with us? We'll have an indoor cook-out—it's too cold to eat outside. It won't be any bother for Moms, 'cause we'll do the work."

"I'm so hungry I don't care *where* we eat," Mart said, "just so we eat!"

Honey and Jim didn't need any more coaxing. Crabapple Farm was a happy place, full of noise and laughter. Honey thought of it as her second home, and she and Jim always enjoyed being with the Beldens.

"We're convinced," Honey said with a smile. "I'll call Miss Trask from there."

"Moms," Trixie called, leading the way into the big kitchen, "Honey and Jim are going to eat dinner with us. We'll have an indoor cookout right here in the kitchen, okay? You go in the living room and relax with Dad—we'll get everything ready, so you won't have a thing to worry about."

Mart and Honey prepared a big salad while Jim took charge of broiling the hot dogs. Brian rushed around, getting in everyone's way, setting the long kitchen table. Trixie peeled potatoes and chopped little white onions for hot potato salad.

Mart breathed deeply as the kitchen filled with appetizing smells. He leaned against the counter and closed his eyes. "Hurry," he urged. "Rigor mortis is setting in!"

When everything was ready, Mr. and Mrs. Belden and Bobby were called to the table. In the center of the bright red and white checked tablecloth was a steaming platter of hot dogs and toasted buns. The big wooden salad bowl was on one side of the table, and on the other side was a serving bowl heaped with hot potato salad. Catsup, mustard, and relish were close at hand.

"Hey!" Bobby exclaimed. "A picnic!"

"The best kind of picnic," Trixie's father pointed out. "No ants!"

Everyone laughed and took a place at the table.

Between mouthfuls, Bobby told his mother and father about surprising the Bob-Whites with his riding ability. "Trixie and me rode to a secret place deep in the woods," he said, "and a car scared Mr. Pony and he ran away."

Mr. Belden looked questioningly at Trixie.

"The old dead-end road behind the game preserve," Trixie explained. "Regan told us that some kids have been using it for drag racing. Mr. Pony didn't go far, and no one got hurt."

"I wasn't riding on Mr. Pony when he ran away," Bobby said quickly. "He was *parked*."

This brought more laughter.

"Well, I'm glad no one got hurt," Mrs. Belden said. "You be careful, young man," she told Bobby, "and ride only in the pasture unless Trixie or the others can ride with you."

After finishing off a chocolate layer cake for dessert, the young people helped clean up the kitchen, and then everyone relaxed around the fireplace in the living room and listened to WSTH.

"Boy," Brian said, "that big band sound is really kind of neat."

"Yeah," Mart admitted. "But I wonder how they did it without any electric guitars."

Peter Belden raised an eyebrow. "Don't any of you have any homework assignments for tomorrow?" he asked.

"Gleeps!" Trixie said. "I've got to finish my social studies report."

"Me, too," Honey said.

Jim nodded. "And we just got through telling Regan that there was no chance of any of us flunking out of school. I guess we'd better prove it. See you guys tomorrow . . . and thanks for the great indoor cookout!"

On the way upstairs, Trixie noticed Mart's puzzled expression. "What's your problem?" she asked.

"I was just wondering who invented the electric guitar," he said.

"That's easy," Trixie said with a grin. "It was Ben Franklin!"

Sam, Sam, the Medicine Man • 3

THE SCHOOL BUS was bouncing down Glen Road, and
Trixie, her notebook balanced on top of her other
books, was trying to keep her handwriting legible.
It wasn't easy—the bus made frequent stops and
starts, and Trixie's paper had streaks and blots where
her pen had shot off suddenly in an unintended
direction.

"Almost finished?" Honey asked, glancing anxiously
at Trixie's messy paper.

Closing her notebook, Trixie sighed. "All done except for sketching in the coins."

Brian looked up from a book he was reading. "What kind of a paper are you doing, anyway?" he asked.

"We have to write a report on the culture of one of the groups of people we've been studying," Trixie told him. "I'm doing the Chinese. They've really got an interesting culture."

"I'm doing the Romans," Honey said.

Trixie looked smug. "We're both going to include sketches of some of the old coins from Mr. Quinn's collection," she boasted. "That's Honey's idea, not mine," she added truthfully.

Honey gave Trixie a poke. "You didn't have to tell him that," she said.

The bus pulled up in front of the school, and the young people gathered up their books and started down the aisle toward the door.

"Using drawings of those coins sounds like a good idea," Brian said. "They should add a lot to your reports."

Trixie nodded. "Now all we have to do is to talk Miss Lawler into letting us stay after class so we can sketch them," she fretted.

The warning bell sounded as they entered the

building. Trixie and Honey hurried off to their home-room. Di and the others ran down the corridor to their own homerooms.

"See you at lunch," Trixie called.

Unlike most Mondays, this one passed quickly. *Jeepers, today seemed short,* Trixie thought as she walked down the hallway to her last class.

Miss Craven was standing by the open door, and she nodded as Trixie entered the social studies class-room. Trixie slipped into her seat beside Honey and arranged her books on her desk as the bell rang to signal the start of class.

Miss Craven closed the door promptly. "Good af-ternoon, class," she said, walking to the front of the room. "Miss Lawler will begin by telling us about another one of the fascinating coins from Mr. Quinn's collection."

Miss Lawler was seated at a small table that served as her desk. A glass display case with a nameplate engraved RONALD QUINN stood beside the table. The sliding glass doors across the back of the case were locked. Inside, the three shelves were covered with black velvet. Laid out in neat rows was an assort-ment of ancient coins—Roman, Greek, Oriental, Hebrew—all of different shapes and sizes. Some were

so blackened with age that they were almost unrec-
ognizable. Many were sealed inside special plastic
envelopes.

While Miss Lawler described one of the coins and
told about the people who had used it, Miss Craven
busied herself taking attendance and looking over
her own notes.

"Thank you, Miss Lawler. Now, class. . . ." Miss
Craven folded her hands and leaned forward. "Today
we'll discuss an ancient Roman city."

The remainder of the period was spent learning
the fascinating story of the excavation of the famous
city of Pompeii.

Trixie didn't even hear the bell sounding to end
the period. She was strolling through the gardens of
Pompeii, admiring the houses, the public baths, and
the great halls and theaters.

Honey giggled and nudged Trixie. "Class is over,"
she informed her.

"Oh!" Blinking her eyes, Trixie looked around at
the other students leaving the room. "Jeepers, that
was really interesting," she said.

"Let's ask Miss Lawler about sketching the coins,"
Honey urged. "She's still at her desk, reading a letter, but she'll probably be leaving as soon as she's
finished."

Picking up her books, Trixie hurried up the aisle to the front of the room. "Miss Lawler," she said, "we were wondering if. . . ."

The teacher's aide looked up quickly, and her eyes were shining with a smile. "Oh, Trixie and Honey. I thought everyone had gone." She slipped the note she had been reading back inside the envelope. "Did you want something?"

Trixie explained what they had in mind. "We wondered if we could stay after class someday when you'll be here," she finished.

"That's a very good idea," Miss Lawler said. "How about tomorrow afternoon? We won't be able to open the case, but you can get a good close look at the coins and the little cards that tell about them."

"That would be terrific," Trixie said gratefully.

"I'll have Jim drive in and pick us up at Wimpy's tomorrow after we're through," Honey suggested to Trixie.

Outside, the bus driver gave two beeps of the horn, signaling that he was ready to leave.

"We have to run," Trixie said. "See you tomorrow, and thanks a lot."

The following afternoon, Trixie and Honey remained in their seats as the other students filed out

48

of the social studies classroom. Miss Craven gathered up her papers, nodded to the girls, and left.

Miss Lawler, seated at her desk, looked up from the papers she was grading. "Take as long as you like," she said. "The cards beside the coins tell quite a bit about them, but if you need some help, just ask."

Trixie and Honey pulled chairs up close to the display case and opened their social studies notebooks in their laps.

Trixie studied the coins spread out on the velvet-covered shelves for a few minutes, chewing on her pencil while she read the information on the cards beside them.

Honey was drawing one of the coins. Beside the drawing, she wrote, *This Roman coin was found in India, showing that there was trade going on between the Roman Empire and India.*

Trixie's pencil flew over the page as she drew a fish, a knife, and a small jacket. *The first Chinese coins were made in shapes of things used for barter,* she wrote beside the drawings.

Looking in the case again, Trixie saw a small triangular coin with a little bell-like thing dangling in the middle.

"Isn't that coin pretty?" Trixie asked, pointing it

49

out to Honey. "It's called—" she leaned closer to read the card— "tingle-tangle, or sometimes, tingle-dangle."

Miss Lawler looked up from her papers. "That's one of my favorites," she said. "In addition to using them for money, the Chinese people also used them as musical instruments. They may also have hung them up as musical mobiles, tingle-tangling in the wind."

"Tingle-tangle," Trixie said softly. "It does sound like music, doesn't it? My little brother Bobby would sure like to see—"

Suddenly Miss Lawler seemed to tremble slightly. Her face turned as white as chalk as she picked up her pencil.

"Are—are you all right, Miss Lawler?" Honey asked quickly.

The teacher's aide pressed her fingers against her forehead. "It's nothing," she said. "I'm . . . rather tired. It's been a long day."

Trixie looked at her watch. "Gosh," she exclaimed, "we've kept you for almost an hour. I'm finished. How about you, Honey?"

Honey nodded. "Just done."

The color was returning to Miss Lawler's face, and she smiled weakly. "I was . . . uh, ill a while ago,"

50

she said, "and I—I tire easily. But please, don't tell anyone what I've told you."

Trixie saw a strange look in Miss Lawler's eyes. Was it fear? Loneliness? Trixie wondered.

Honey picked up her notebook. "We won't mention it to anyone—anyone at all," she assured the teacher's aide.

"That's a promise," Trixie said.

"Thank you," Miss Lawler murmured. "Good night, now."

Still puzzling over the scene in the classroom, Trixie and Honey walked across the lawn to the sidewalk and headed toward downtown to meet Jim at Wimpy's.

"I guess Miss Lawler is afraid," Trixie said after a moment. "She's afraid of being sick again."

"I know how she feels," Honey said softly. "I used to feel that way, too, until we moved to Sleepyside and I met you and all the other Bob-Whites."

"I wish we could help her," Trixie sighed.

"How about helping me?" someone asked.

Startled, both girls looked up to see a young man, leaning against a battered old yellow pickup truck, grinning at them. He seemed to be about Brian's age, tall and slender, with curly black hair and a friendly, likable smile.

"I'm looking for Miss Lawler," he said. "She's supposed to be at the Sleepyside High School. Am I in the right place?"

"You sure are!" Trixie and Honey answered in one voice.

"We were just with her," Honey said.

"She's still in her classroom," Trixie added. "We'll show you the way."

"Thanks!" The young man followed them into the school building, walking with a loose, easy stride.

Moments later, they were standing at the classroom door. "Someone to see you, Miss Lawler," Trixie called.

Miss Lawler was covering the display case. "Just a moment," she said. Turning, she saw the young man. "Why, Sammy!" she cried. "I didn't expect to see you so soon."

Grinning, the young man crossed the room. "Hi, Cis," he said.

Miss Lawler was obviously delighted. "I got your letter," she said in a rush, "but—"

Honey nudged Trixie and whispered, "Come on." Quietly, she and Trixie stepped down the hallway toward the exit.

Outside, Trixie laughed and said, "How about *that*? Miss Lawler really looked happy!"

"His name is Sammy," Honey mused. She was as excited as Trixie.

"Sam, Sam, the Medicine Man," Trixie chanted. "Gleeps! He's just what the doctor ordered!"

The Mysterious Car • 4

JIM AND THE OTHER BOB-WHITES had driven into town to pick up Trixie and Honey. Now they were all seated in their favorite booth at Wimpy's, sipping colas and listening to Trixie describe the happy scene she and Honey had just witnessed. Her excitement was contagious.

"It sounds wonderful," Di said with a sigh.

"Sure, it's great," Mart agreed. "And for once, Trixie has met somebody new and not said—"

"There's something strange about him!" the others chimed in, laughing.

"Who is this Sammy, anyway?" Brian asked.

"Well," Trixie said matter-of-factly, "he called Miss Lawler Sis, so he must be her brother."

Di, who sat facing the door, leaned forward and whispered, "Shhh! They just came in here. They're coming over this way."

Honey turned her head and smiled. "Hi, Miss Lawler," she called.

Trixie moved over on the bench, making space beside her. "Come sit with us," she invited. "There's room for two more."

The teacher's aide was pleased. "Why, thank you," she said, stopping by the crowded booth, "but—"

"Sure," Sammy said. "Sit down, Cis." Sammy slid into the booth beside Trixie. "Hi," he said, nodding to the other Bob-Whites. "My name's Sammy."

"I'm Trixie Belden, and this is Honey Wheeler. We sort of met you in front of school," Trixie said. She introduced each of the others at the table. "We're the Bob-Whites," she told him.

"That's the name of their club, Sammy," Miss Lawler explained. "They're all good friends of mine."

Sammy shrugged. "Then they're all good friends of mine, too," he said.

Sammy seemed to be an easy person to know. He had a great sense of humor and a droll way of telling stories—most of them about his own misadventures. In a few minutes, he had everyone at the table howling with laughter.

"Sammy, if you're going to be staying in Sleepyside, you'll *have* to join the Drama Club at school," Trixie said, weak from laughing.

"School?" Sammy asked in a sarcastic tone. "Forget it. That's almost as bad as being locked up. I'm nineteen, and I'm finished with school, that's for sure."

"Sammy's just taking some time off to travel a bit," Miss Lawler said quickly. "Next year, he'll be entering college."

"Maybe," Sammy said. Then he smiled. "I'm glad Cis wrote and told me about Sleepyside," he went on, changing the subject. "Finding little old towns like this is sort of a hobby with me. I like to keep on the move. I just got here today, but I already think Sleepyside is one of the neatest places I've hit yet."

The Bob-Whites nodded proudly. "We think Sleepyside is great," Trixie said.

"Are you going to be staying here awhile?" Mart queried.

"I hope so," Miss Lawler answered for Sammy.

"Look," Sammy said impatiently, "I told you I didn't come here to sponge off you, Cis."

Miss Lawler bent her head and took a quick sip of her cola. The others remained uncomfortably silent for a moment.

Sammy smiled again. "We'll see," he said. "I'll stick around for a while, anyway."

"We'd better *not* stick around here any longer," Trixie said. "I promised Moms we'd be on time for dinner for a change."

Jim buttoned up his red jacket. "Our station wagon is over in the parking lot," he said. "Can we give you and Sammy a lift, Miss Lawler?"

"No, thank you, Jim," Miss Lawler answered. "We left Sammy's truck at the school. We'll walk back there. But—" she smiled suddenly, remembering something— "we will walk down to the common with you. I want Sammy to meet Hoppy."

"Sure," Sammy said agreeably. "I hope Hoppy is as pretty as Di."

Di blushed, and everyone else laughed.

"Hoppy's undeniable pulchritude, however, would undoubtedly appeal more to an orthopteran," Mart said. "He's a grasshopper weather vane atop the cupola of our Town Hall."

"Don't mind Mart," Trixie said. "He likes to sound

57

like a dictionary. Hoppy is over two hundred years old. He's a real antique."

Miss Lawler nodded. "Tell Sammy the part about the good luck, Trixie," she said.

"Oh," Trixie said self-consciously. "We—I mean, some of us—think it brings good luck to say hello to Hoppy whenever you pass him."

Sammy's grin widened. "Is that right?" he asked. "This I've got to see. Lead the way."

The crisp October air felt almost frosty after the cozy warmth of the diner. Trixie shivered and turned up her jacket collar as they headed toward the town common.

They passed a car at the curb, sitting with the motor running. A thin trail of smoke puffed from the exhaust. The man behind the steering wheel was reading a newspaper.

"I don't blame him for leaving his heater on," Trixie muttered. "Jeepers, I'm freezing!" She pushed her hands deep into her pockets, then let out a sudden gasp. "Yipes! I forgot my notebook. I'll run back to the diner and get it. You guys go on; I'll catch up."

The notebook was right where Trixie had left it on the bench.

"Forget something, Trixie?" Mike, the counterman, called to her.

"Practically a whole social studies report!" Trixie told him as she went back out the door. "See you later, Mike."

Trixie could see the others almost at the common. She started to run to catch up, but then slowed down. The car they had passed before was inching along, close to the curb, keeping just behind the group on the sidewalk. *I wonder who that is,* Trixie thought. She yelled, "Hey, you guys! Wait for me!"

As the others turned around, the car pulled away from the curb and drove off.

Honey waited until Trixie caught up with her. The others were already walking across the grass of the common.

"Did you notice that car that just passed?" Trixie asked Honey.

"What car?" Honey asked. "We were too busy talking to be looking at cars. Why? Who was it?"

Trixie frowned. "I don't know. But it seemed to be following you."

"Oh, Trixie!" Honey chided. "It was probably just someone who doesn't know his way around Sleepyside very well. Come on, the others are waiting for us."

They joined the group in front of Town Hall and watched as Sammy craned his neck to stare up at the old weather vane. In the late afternoon light, the old grasshopper looked almost alive and ready to hop from his perch.

Sammy shook his head. "Now, that's one mighty big grasshopper," he said.

Miss Lawler touched Sammy's arm. "Don't forget that it's good luck to say hello to Hoppy," she reminded him.

"Right," Sammy said. With a mock salute, he called, "Hello, Hoppy! You're the biggest bug I've ever seen! And I think you're going to bring me a lot of good luck!"

Miss Lawler laughed. "He'll bring you a parking ticket if we don't get back to your truck," she said.

Trixie looked at her watch and made a face. "We've got to get home!" she said. "It was nice meeting you, Sammy. Good night, Miss Lawler."

The Bob-Whites headed for their station wagon, and Miss Lawler and Sammy started off up the sidewalk toward the school building.

"Miss Lawler seems like a different person already," Trixie declared as Jim drove home. "Remember how nervous and shy she used to be?"

"Sammy really changed that," Honey said. "I wish we could convince him to stay in Sleepyside. Maybe if we knew of a job for him . . . but there aren't any job openings at Manor House now. What about your family, Di?"

Di shook her head. "We need a maid," she said, "but somehow I don't think Sammy would be interested in that."

"Think, everybody," Trixie ordered. "Let's make it a club project to find a job for Sammy somewhere in Sleepyside."

"Okay," Jim agreed. "We'll become regular readers of the want ads."

Mrs. Belden was setting the table when Trixie, Brian, and Mart came into the kitchen.

"Sorry we're late, Moms," Trixie said, taking the silverware from her. "Here, I'll finish that."

Mart lifted the lid from a pot on the stove and sniffed. "Ahh," he said, "satisfaction for my olfaction. What is it, Moms?"

"It's braised beef," his mother told him, "and you put that lid right back on the pot, Mart Belden."

Trixie looked up and wrinkled her nose. "I smell green apple pie, too," she said with a grin.

Her mother laughed. "My daughter, the detective," she said. "And I thought I had that pie well hidden."

Bobby came in from the living room. "Hi, everybody!" he shouted. "What kept you so long, Trixie?"

Trixie went on folding the napkins and putting them in place. "It's a long story, Bobby," she said. "We'll tell you about it while we eat."

During dinner, Trixie and the boys told their parents what had happened that afternoon. "Oh, Moms," Trixie said with eyes sparkling, "I wish you could have seen Miss Lawler. She's so happy now that her brother is here."

"Sammy really does seem like a nice guy," Brian said.

"And he can sure tell a story," Mart added.

Trixie grew wistful. "I just hope he can find a job in town," she said. "It would be so good for Miss Lawler to have him stay. We were hoping that the Wheelers or the Lynches might have something for him, but they don't."

Peter Belden rubbed his chin. "I know where Sammy might find a job," he said slowly. "I was talking to Mr. Johnson, the Town Hall custodian, in the bank today. He said the town council has authorized him to hire someone to help him. The outside work is getting to be too much for him. He just finished painting the building, but the roof needs work, too, and the weather vane is loose. Maybe Sammy—"

"Gleeps!" Trixie exclaimed. "Hoppy's brought Sammy good luck already! I'm sure he'd be just right for the job. We don't know where Sammy is staying, but I'll tell Miss Lawler about the job first thing in the morning."

Brian looked at Mart. "Maybe *we* should start saying hello to Hoppy," he said.

"I'd rather say hello to another helping of potatoes, please," Mart replied.

The Walk-a-thon Plan • 5

TRIXIE RUSHED into the social studies classroom first thing the following morning, tingling with excitement. "Hoppy's brought good luck," she told Miss Lawler. She explained about Mr. Johnson needing a helper at Town Hall. "I told Dad I was sure that Sammy could do it. Would he like that kind of work?"

The teacher's aide smiled and nodded. "Indeed he would," she answered. "Sammy is very good at maintenance work—painting, repairing, building. He was always doing something like that at the house. He's quite skillful."

"That's terrific," Trixie said. "I made Dad promise to call Mr. Johnson this morning and tell him about Sammy. Could you call Sammy right now, before classes begin, and tell him to go to Town Hall and see Mr. Johnson?"

The happy expression faded from Miss Lawler's face. "Sammy isn't staying with me," she said. "He's rented a room somewhere, and he doesn't have a phone."

"Oh," Trixie said, disappointed.

"Wait a minute!" Miss Lawler said, opening her purse and searching for something. "He did give me a number to call where I could leave a message for him," she recalled. "Ah, here it is!"

"Call right now," Trixie urged, starting out the door. "I'll bet he gets the job," she added confidently.

That afternoon, as Trixie and Honey entered their social studies class, one look at Miss Lawler's face told them Trixie had been right.

As the girls passed her desk, Miss Lawler said, "Sammy got the job, Trixie. Thank you, and please give our thanks to your father, too."

Trixie grinned. "I knew Sammy would get the job,"

she said. "Now he can stay in Sleepyside."

Miss Craven closed the door and crossed to her desk. "Good afternoon, class," she greeted them. "Trixie, Honey, take your seats, please. We're ready to begin."

As they walked to their desks, Trixie whispered, "Wait till we tell the other Bob-Whites about this!"

Later that afternoon, Jim rapped the gavel on the table in the Bob-White clubhouse. "The meeting will come to order," he announced in his most official-sounding tone.

The six other Bob-Whites stopped talking and sat down in their assigned places around the table. Trixie took her place beside Jim.

The clubhouse was warm and snug, decorated in cheerful colors and comfortably furnished. It bore little resemblance to the broken-down gatehouse it had been. Trixie and Honey had discovered it at the edge of the Wheeler property, overgrown with vines and bushes. With the Wheelers' permission, the Bob-Whites had all worked to clean and repair the gatehouse and transform it into a perfect clubhouse.

Jim scanned the agenda for the meeting. "First thing on our schedule is a vote of thanks to Trixie," he said.

The others looked questioningly at Trixie. She reddened with embarrassment.

Jim smiled. "Trixie helped to get Sammy a job at Town Hall," he declared, "so he'll be staying in Sleepyside, close to Miss Lawler. There's one club project completed in record time."

"That's wonderful," Di said.

"Great!" Brian exclaimed. Everyone clapped.

"Mr. Copresident," Mart called out, "I note that a certain member of the club is still in violation of our punctilious appearance rule. An unkempt jacket reflects an unfavorable image of our club, hence I call attention to the right jacket sleeve of Miss Beatrix Belden."

Jim turned his head to hide his smile, then coughed and answered pompously. "Thank you, Mr. Secretary-Treasurer," he said. "Violation is duly noted. And since it was first pointed out on Saturday, said violator now owes the club treasury fifty cents—ten cents a day."

The clubhouse erupted with laughter. Trixie tried hard, but she couldn't keep from laughing herself. "Gleeps!" she said. "I forgot all about the button. I looked for it on Sunday, honest!"

"Well, it's not in here," Mart said, holding out the cashbox. "Fifty cents, please."

Suddenly Trixie's eyes widened in disbelief. "Mr. Copresident," she announced, "I would like to point out another member of the club who is also in violation of the punk—punkta—whatever that rule is. Look closely, and you'll see a spot of catsup on the jacket of the secretary-treasurer."

"Where?" Mart yelled, jumping to his feet. "Show me!"

"Right there, Mart," Honey said, pointing to a dark red spot on the front of the bright red jacket.

"Yikes!" Mart looked at the spot. "How did that get there?"

"Well, it didn't come from here," Trixie said, dropping her fine into the box and holding it out to her brother. "Pay up, Mart," she ordered.

"*Nolo contendere*," Mart acknowledged wryly as he dug in his pocket for a dime and dropped it in the box.

Jim rapped for order. "We may have another club project to contend with now," he said, looking over the agenda. "Trixie told me about it, and she'll explain it now."

Trixie was serious at once. "When Dad told me about Mr. Johnson needing a helper, he also said something about Hoppy. Mr. Johnson says that Hoppy needs to be replated with new copper. Other-

68

wise, the weather vane may be damaged by the weather this winter. The town council has given Mr. Johnson money to repair the roof, but there isn't enough money to have Hoppy recoppered, too. That means Hoppy may have to be taken down from his perch—permanently."

"No more good luck," Mart teased, but his tone held regret.

"Town Hall just won't be the same without Hoppy on top," Di said.

"Di's right," Trixie agreed. "I think that a worthy project for the Bob-Whites would be to help raise the money to have Hoppy recoppered."

"That's a good idea," Dan said quickly. The others nodded.

Di looked worried. "But what can we do?" she asked. "We've already given a winter carnival and had an antique sale. How else can we raise the money?"

"How about a walk-a-thon?" Trixie suggested. "We've never tried that before."

Brian was interested at once. "I like that idea," he said. "We could get a lot of people from school to volunteer as walkers, and set up a course through town with special checkpoints at various places along the way—"

"Good," Trixie said. "But first we have to find some sponsors—businesses, or just people who are interested—to pledge a certain amount of money for every mile someone walks. And we need some good publicity before we begin."

"I have an idea!" Honey exclaimed. "My father is a good friend of Mr. Perkins, who owns WSTH. Maybe he'd announce it on his radio station for us."

"Great!" Trixie said. "Your dad can help us solve that problem."

The Bob-Whites spent the rest of the meeting making further plans for the walk-a-thon.

On the way back to Crabapple Farm, Trixie sighed. "I wish I could get good ideas for my social studies report as easily as I do for club projects," she said.

"I thought you finished that report," Brian said.

"It's almost done now," Trixie admitted. "I have to make a couple more drawings of coins, that's all. Honey and I are going to stay after school for a while tomorrow. We'll come home in a cab."

After social studies class the following afternoon, Trixie and Honey talked with some classmates in the hall and asked for their help with the walk-a-thon. When the hall had emptied, they returned to the classroom to work on their reports.

"I'll be here for a while," Miss Lawler said. "Ask if you need help." She went to work on a stack of test papers.

Pulling chairs close to the case, the girls examined the ancient coins once more. Honey quickly located an old Roman coin she needed and began sketching, but Trixie puzzled over one row of Chinese coins for several minutes.

There were a great many round copper coins with holes in the middle. "They all look alike to me," Trixie muttered softly.

"But they're not," someone said in her ear.

"Oh!" Trixie jumped. "Sammy!" she said. "You startled me."

"Sorry," Sammy said earnestly. "I came to see Cis. I'm glad to find you here, though. I want to thank you and your father for helping me get my job at Town Hall. Cis told me that your dad put in a good word for me, and I sure appreciate it. You'll never know how much you've helped me."

Trixie reddened. Being thanked for doing something good made her feel uncomfortable. "That's okay," she said with a shrug. "We're glad you got the job."

"Sammy," Miss Lawler said, "why don't you help Trixie with those Chinese coins. She's using some of them in a report on Chinese culture. I'm sure you can help her."

Seeing the surprised expressions of Trixie and Honey, Miss Lawler explained. "Sammy's a pretty accomplished numismatist. He was interested, so I taught him everything I know about coins."

"That's neat," Trixie said. "Do you collect coins, too, Sammy?" she asked.

"Why, sure," Sammy said with a sneer, his voice suddenly sounding bitter. "All of us rich people collect coins. I carry my coin collection right here in my pocket." Roughly he pulled out a coin. "Look," he said, "a buffalo nickel! Vereee valuable. I scratched my initials into it so no coin thieves would get it. See?"

"Sammy—" Miss Lawler began.

But Sammy's old grin was back. Returning the coin to his pocket, he said, "You don't mind a little music while you work, do you?" He lifted a transistor radio from his shirt pocket and turned it on. "I'm a rock music freak," he admitted.

For the next half hour, Trixie kept Sammy busy answering questions about the row of round coins.

"Why do some have a round hole in the middle and others have a square hole?" she asked.

Sammy explained that the ancient Chinese had

found their copper supply getting low. Their coins were made from copper, and they needed more coins, so apparently they decided to cut the middle out of one coin to make two! Their original coins had a small square hole in the center. So when they cut the centers out, they had one small coin with a square hole in the middle and a somewhat larger coin with a circular hole in the middle.

Trixie was fascinated. She made careful drawings of the two types of coins.

"Now look at that one," she said, pointing to another coin in the row. "That doesn't have any hole at all. How come?"

"That's a more modern Chinese coin," Sammy told her. "Chinese coins have no holes in them now."

"Okay," Trixie said, closing her notebook. "I've got everything I need for my report now. How about you, Honey?"

Honey laughed. "I finished a long time ago," she said. "I've just been listening to Sammy."

Sammy wiped his brow as if he had been laboring strenuously. "Whew! I'm glad I'm not a teacher," he said. "That's *work!*"

Miss Lawler smiled and covered the display case with the green felt dustcover. "Sammy, why don't you drive Trixie and Honey home?" she suggested.

"I'll walk down to the diner, and you can meet me there."

"We've bothered Sammy enough today," Honey said quickly. "Trixie and I can call a cab."

Sammy laughed. "No problem. I'll be happy to take you guys home, *if* you don't mind riding in my old truck. Come on."

Sammy's yellow pickup looked old and dilapidated, but surprisingly, the engine was smooth and powerful, and the ride was almost as good as that of the Bob-White station wagon.

Trixie spoke loudly against the volume of the radio. "I never knew a truck could ride like this."

For answer, Sammy speeded up, ignoring the speed limit signs. "It doesn't look like much, but it goes," he bragged.

Trixie was glad to see her driveway up ahead. "Turn there," she said in plenty of time for Sammy to slow down. "You can drop me off first. Honey's house is up on the hill."

Seconds later, Trixie was climbing down from the high cab seat of the truck. "Thanks for the ride—and the coin lesson," she said.

The truck was already moving again. "My pleasure," Sammy called back, backing down the driveway at a fast speed.

That's funny, Trixie thought, walking to the door. *Sammy said he was a rock music freak, but the radio in the truck was playing old-fashioned music. Must have been WSTH.*

That Car Again • 6

Moms, have you seen the gold button that belongs on my Bob-White jacket?" Trixie asked on the following afternoon.

Mrs. Belden looked up from the warm ginger cookies she had just taken from the oven. "It was on your night table," she said.

Trixie sighed. "I know. But it's not there now. You know what?" she asked, helping herself to a cookie.

"I'm positive that Bobby has it in his button collection at the tree house."

Mrs. Belden nodded. "I wouldn't be surprised," she said shrewdly.

"Oh, Moms," Trixie rushed on, "I know it's Friday afternoon, but could I please be excused from the dusting, just—"

"—this once," her mother completed the familiar phrase. Then she laughed. "Go ahead, Trixie," she said, "but you'll have to hurry. I don't like your being in the woods by yourself, and it's getting dark early these days."

"Bobby's tree house isn't deep in the woods, Moms," Trixie reminded her. "The old road is just on the other side of the trees."

"I know." Her mother slid the next batch of cookies into the oven. "Be sure to take your flashlight, though."

Trixie was already at the door. "I have it right here," she said with a grin. "I won't be long."

A few minutes later, Trixie was jogging along at a steady pace, headed into the woods. She remembered the exact location of the tree house, but getting there on foot took quite a bit longer than getting there on horseback.

The sun was almost gone when Trixie finally reached her destination and climbed up into the little tree house.

Bobby's treasures were lined up on the floor in boxes and tin cans. Trixie sat down and carefully spread the button collection out at her feet. "Colored buttons, plain buttons, wooden buttons, and—jeepers, a black shoe button! That's from my old Raggedy Ann doll." Trixie mumbled to herself as she sorted through the collection. One by one, she let the buttons drop with a *clink* back into the tin. "And here, at last, is my Bob-White button!" she said. "No more fines!"

With a sigh of relief, Trixie tucked the gold metal button into her pocket and returned the others to the tin. As she stood, she saw a flash of light through the trees beside the old road.

"There must be a car driving on that road again," Trixie said to herself. Peering through the branches, she spotted the car, coming along the old road. "Hey!" Trixie breathed. "That's the same car that I saw following everyone a few nights ago!"

She observed the car pulling to a stop. The driver climbed out and stood for a moment, looking around. Then he crossed in front of the car to examine the faded road sign. In the glare of the headlights, Trixie could see that he was tall and strong-looking, with dark hair cut close to his head.

What's he looking for? Trixie wondered, watching as the man returned to his car.

It was quite dark now. Trixie cupped her hand around her flashlight and climbed down from the tree. As her feet touched the ground, she slipped on the leaves and fell with a clatter of breaking twigs. Her flashlight flew from her hand, shooting a beam of light out to the trees near the road.

"Hey! Who's there?" the man beside the car shouted.

Without looking back, Trixie grabbed her flashlight, scrambled to her feet, and raced down the path toward Crabapple Farm.

Mrs. Belden was at the stove, stirring her special sauce for the turkey cutlets, when Trixie entered the warm, bright kitchen.

"Is that you, Trixie?" her mother asked, without looking up from her cooking. "You're just in time to drain the vegetables and butter them. I can't leave the sauce now."

"Okay, Moms," Trixie said, hoping she didn't sound out of breath and frightened.

"Did you find the button you were looking for?" her mother asked.

"Yes, I did," Trixie answered. "And I'm going to sew it on right after dinner, before Bobby has a chance to 'collect' it again."

"Let's hope he hasn't collected all of my thread," Mrs. Belden said with a chuckle.

After helping clean up the dinner dishes, Trixie got a needle and some red thread from her mother's sewing box and sat on the living room floor beneath a lamp. After several tries at threading the needle, she finally succeeded and went to work sewing the button into place on her jacket sleeve.

Brian was stretched out on the floor nearby, reading a magazine. "It's a good thing Honey volunteered to make our jackets," he remarked. "If Trix was doing it, I'm afraid we'd all get pretty chilly waiting for them."

"She's merely heeding what Ben Franklin said about sewing," Mart said.

"And what was that, young man?" Mr. Belden asked with a raised eyebrow.

"Haste to baste makes waste," Mart recited with an impish grin.

80

Everyone winced.

"Well," Trixie countered, "I'll bet that Ben Franklin could eat a hamburger without getting catsup on *his* jacket!"

"Touché," Mart said. "I forgot about that. Moms, how do I get a catsup stain out of my jacket?"

"The same way I get the catsup stains out of all your clothes," Mrs. Belden advised. "Use some spot remover first, and then soap and water."

Mart hurried off.

"Speaking of Honey," Trixie said, "I'm going to call her and ask how her social studies report is coming."

Actually, Trixie couldn't wait to tell Honey about what she had seen at the tree house. Dialing quickly, she soon heard Honey's voice at the other end of the line. "Do you remember Tuesday night, when I saw a car following you?" she asked.

"I remember you said something about a car . . . someone not knowing his way around Sleepyside," Honey said.

"*You* said it was somebody who didn't know his way around," Trixie said. "But I'm sure that car was following you. And I saw that very same car again tonight."

"Really? Where?"

Trixie told about going to Bobby's tree house to look for her jacket button. "The man got out of the car and looked around," she said. "What do you suppose he was doing poking around that old dead-end road?"

"Maybe he *still* doesn't know his way around," Honey said.

"Hmmm," Trixie said skeptically. "Well, I think something is up. I'm going to keep an eye out for that car. See you tomorrow afternoon?"

"Right," Honey said.

Saturday was overcast and windy. When the Bob-Whites went riding, the horses seemed unusually nervous and skittish.

On Sunday, the young people met at the clubhouse to make more plans for the walk-a-thon. The wind had been growing stronger all day, and though it was only early afternoon, the threatening sky was almost black.

"I think we'd better adjourn early," Jim said as the first big raindrops began to spatter on the windows. "It looks like this is going to be a pretty good storm. See you on the bus tomorrow."

Jacket collars turned up against the wind, Trixie, Brian, and Mart hurried home. Their father was waiting for them at the back door. "I was just about to come and get you!" he shouted against the force of the wind. "There's been a severe storm warning posted. Everyone is to stay indoors and have candles ready in case of a power failure."

"Let's have dinner before the lights go out," Mart urged. "I like to see what I'm eating."

While everyone helped set the table for dinner, the rain came in heavy waves, drumming against the side of the snug old house. Tree branches scraped and bumped against the roof. With a loud *crack!* a branch broke off one of the trees and crashed to the ground.

As they were eating dessert, the lights flickered and went out.

"Hey!" Bobby yelled angrily. "Who turned off the lights?"

"It's all right, Bobby," Mr. Belden said calmly. "The power lines are down." In a minute he had the old gas lamp lit. "We probably won't have any electricity until tomorrow," he said.

"We'll have to watch television with the lights off," Bobby complained.

"No television, either," Mr. Belden said, mussing Bobby's hair.

"No television?" Bobby wailed in dismay. "What will we *do?*"

"Let's do what they did in the old days," Trixie said cheerfully. "We'll play games and sing songs by candlelight. It'll be fun!"

"Those 'old days' weren't all that long ago," Mrs. Belden pointed out wryly. "Maybe a night without electricity will do us all good."

"Yeah," Mart agreed. "Look what it did for Ben Franklin!"

Sitting around a roaring fire in the living room, the whole family played guessing games, told jokes, and sang songs. Mrs. Belden reeled off a string of tongue twisters that amazed everyone. She challenged the young people to match her skill, and the results had everyone doubled over with laughter.

When it was time for Bobby to go to bed, he said, "I like the old days! We get to tell jokes and sing songs just like they do on television."

"Maybe we *should* start a family television show," Brian said.

"I think a family circus would be more our style," Mr. Belden said with a smile.

Later, Trixie snuggled in bed and listened to the sounds of the storm outside. *Poor old Hoppy,* she thought with a shudder. *I hope the storm doesn't damage him.*

Where Is Hoppy? • 7

THE MORNING SUN shining on her face woke Trixie.
Swinging out of bed, she stretched and then bent and
touched her toes. "No more storm," she said, seeing
blue sky from her window.

The yard was littered with broken tree branches
and piles of soggy leaves. The heavy limb from the
shade tree lay crumpled beside the trunk. There were
pools of dirty water everywhere.

"Gleeps, what a mess," Trixie moaned. "I wonder

if the electricity is back on." A snap of the light switch told her that the power had been restored. "No holiday from school," Trixie said with a shake of her head.

After making her bed and dressing, Trixie went down to breakfast. The rest of the family was already at the kitchen table, listening to the radio.

Trixie slipped into her place beside Bobby. "Smells good, Moms," she said, taking her plate from her mother.

"My favorite fruit," Mart sighed between bites. "Hot pancakes with melted butter and maple syrup."

Trixie widened her eyes. "That's a surprise," she said. "I thought your favorite fruit grew on a hamburger tree."

Mart helped himself to more syrup and nodded. "That's my favorite *dinner* fruit," he explained. "This is my favorite *breakfast* fruit."

"Trixie," Bobby said, tugging at her arm, "listen to me. I have something 'portant to tell you. The radio man said the storm broke some of the windows at my school. Does the TV work today, or is it still like the old days?"

"Well," Trixie said, "if the radio works, then the TV set will work, too."

"That's good," Bobby said, " 'cause the radio man

87

said the school windows are broken, and I don't have to go to school today."

"Gee, that's too -bad," Trixie said in mock pity. "How about our school, Dad?" she asked.

Mr. Belden smiled and shook his head. "No such luck, Trixie," he said. "Your school building wasn't damaged at all. Classes as usual today. From what they said on the news, the storm damage isn't really too bad. A lot of tree branches are down, and there's a little flooding in spots. The power was off all night, but they had that fixed early this morning."

Mrs. Belden poured herself more coffee. "Honey called before you came down," she told Trixie. "Some of the roads are blocked with tree limbs, and the school bus will be late getting around, so Jim is driving this morning. He'll come by for all of you in the station wagon."

Trixie looked at the clock and gulped. "I'd better get my books," she said, pushing her chair back from the table. "Thanks for the good breakfast, Moms."

When Trixie and her brothers climbed into the station wagon a few minutes later, Trixie could tell that Honey had some kind of good news.

"Jeepers," Trixie said, "for somebody who didn't get an extra day off from school, you sure look happy this morning."

88

"I am happy," Honey said. "Wait till you hear this! Mr. and Mrs. Perkins were visiting with Mother and Daddy when Jim and I got home yesterday. I told Mr. Perkins about our plans for a walk-a-thon to raise money for recoppering the weather vane, and I asked him if he'd announce the walk-a-thon over WSTH."

"What did he say?" Trixie asked.

Honey looked smug. "Are you ready for this? Mr. Perkins suggested that we all go to the station and make the announcement ourselves! He's arranged a taping session for tomorrow afternoon, right after school."

"Gleeps!" Trixie thumped her hands against the books in her lap. "Honey, that's great!" she said.

"*Mirabile dictu!*" Mart agreed.

Brian shook his head as Trixie glared at Mart. "Honey used to be so shy she could barely say hello," he said, "and now she's going to be on the radio!"

"We can *all* be on the radio," Honey reminded him.

Elated, the young people began making plans. It was agreed unanimously that Mart should write the announcement. There was some good-natured argument about who should actually do the talking.

"Jim—he's the club copresident."

"It was Trixie's idea!"

"But Brian is the best speaker."

"No—Honey should do it. She got permission."

"Wait a minute!" Mart whistled and signaled for time-out. "Let's not tax our brains so severely before school even begins. I suggest we have a meeting after school in the clubhouse."

Everyone agreed.

Jim pulled into a parking space in front of the school building. "End of the line," he called. "All out."

Trixie consulted her watch. "We're twenty minutes early. If Honey and I go to homeroom now, the teacher will put us to work sorting books or something."

"You're right," Honey agreed. "She can always find something to keep everyone busy."

Mart wagged a finger under Honey's nose. "Now, now, Honey—idle hands get into mischief," he reminded her primly.

Honey burst out laughing. "Oh, Mart, you should be a homeroom teacher!" she said.

Trixie had an idea. "Let's drive downtown and see if the storm did any damage," she suggested. "We'll be back in plenty of time."

"Not me," Brian said, getting out of the wagon. "I'm going over to the gym to shoot some baskets."

"I'll join you," Mart said, climbing out.

"We'll see you at noon in the lunchroom," Trixie called as Jim pulled out into the street.

There wasn't much storm damage downtown. The streets had large puddles of water, and there was some debris—mostly newspapers and loose trash can lids. A few of the older trees had lost some branches. Workmen were busy clearing the sidewalks of twigs and muddy leaves.

The big front windows of some of the stores and the newspaper office had been taped for protection from the wind.

Jim drove slowly, and Honey and Trixie checked out both sides of the street.

"The church, the library, the dress shop," Trixie counted off each building as they passed. "Everything looks okay," she said, sounding relieved.

"Town Hall is all right," Honey added as they passed the common. "I was worried about Hoppy last night."

"Me, too," Trixie admitted. "I sure hope we can raise the money to have him replated. Let's not forget to say hello to him today." Trixie poked her head outside the car window.

"Hello, Hop—" she began, then gasped. "Hoppy's not on the roof! He's gone!"

Honey leaned out her window and stared up at the bare cupola.

Jim pulled over to the curb to look for himself. "Mr. Johnson said that the base needed repairs. That wind last night must have knocked Hoppy off his perch."

"Poor Hoppy," Honey sighed.

Trixie was out of the car already, scanning the ground around Town Hall. "I can't see Hoppy anywhere on the ground," she said.

"Maybe he landed on the other side of the building," Honey suggested.

Jim nodded. "That's the direction the wind was blowing last night," he said. "I just hope Hoppy was strong enough to take the fall without being smashed."

Trixie headed around the building. "We'd better go look," she said.

"Trixie, we don't have enough time," Honey warned. "Besides, what would we do with Hoppy if we found him? Town Hall doesn't open until nine o'clock."

Reluctantly, Trixie agreed. "Let's report it to the police, then," she said. "The station is right across the street—it'll only take a minute."

When Trixie hurried into the small police station,

Sergeant Molinson was just sitting down at his desk with a cup of coffee and a doughnut. He looked at Trixie and scowled. "Are you skipping school today, Detective Belden?" he asked.

"Of course not," Trixie replied. "Sergeant Molinson, something awful has happened! We were driving past Town Hall just now, and we noticed that Hoppy isn't up on the roof. The storm must have knocked him down. We don't have time to look for him, so we thought—"

"Who is Hoppy?" Sergeant Molinson interrupted sharply.

"The grasshopper weather vane," Trixie said. "He's been on top of Town Hall since—"

The sergeant was annoyed. Leaning across his desk, he said, "Trixie, crime is my business. I don't have time to go around looking for weather vanes that fall off roofs. Mr. Johnson takes care of Town Hall, so that's his problem, not mine."

Trixie was not put off easily. "Hoppy belongs to everyone in Sleepyside," she said. "That weather vane is part of Sleepyside history—and a valuable antique, too. It can't be left just lying on the ground. Please, Sergeant Molinson?"

Molinson sighed. "I'll check into it," he said.

"Thanks!" Trixie said, rushing out of the police

station. "Let's go," she urged Jim. "The bell rings in five minutes."

Morning classes seemed to drag on endlessly. Trixie tried to concentrate, but her thoughts kept returning to Hoppy. She wondered if he had been found, and whether he was badly damaged from the fall. Luckily, Trixie was not called on to answer questions in class. When the lunch bell finally sounded, she was the first one out the door.

As she rushed down the hall to the lunchroom, Trixie spotted Miss Lawler coming out of her classroom.

"Miss Lawler, wait a minute please," Trixie called.

The teacher's aide looked especially attractive today, Trixie noticed. Her hair was cut in a new fluffy style, and her beige skirt and blouse were fashionable and expensive-looking.

"Hello, Trixie," she said with a smile.

"Have you seen Sammy?" Trixie asked breathlessly.

"Why, no, not today," Miss Lawler answered. "Why?"

Quickly, Trixie told her about Hoppy. "We think the storm knocked him loose from the base. He must have fallen behind the building, but we didn't have time to look for him," she said. Trixie pushed her curly hair back from her face and sighed, "Hoppy's so old that I'm afraid he may be broken."

Miss Lawler bit her lower lip. "I—I'd better call Sammy at Town Hall," she said. "Where's the nearest pay telephone?"

Trixie pointed to the far end of the corridor. "Right down there," she said. "Please come over to our lunch table and tell us if you hear any news from Sammy."

The Bob-Whites were waiting for Trixie at their usual table in the lunchroom.

"Has everyone heard the news?" Trixie asked as she sat down beside Di and began her lunch.

"We all know," Brian said. "Honey and Jim told us about Hoppy."

Trixie took a bite of her tuna fish sandwich. "I just told Miss Lawler about it, and she's calling Sammy at Town Hall. If there's any news, she'll tell us."

"Here she comes now," Dan said, seeing the teacher's aide crossing the room.

As soon as Miss Lawler reached their table, Trixie asked anxiously, "Did you talk to Sammy?"

Miss Lawler shook her head from side to side. "I spoke with Mr. Johnson," she answered. "He said Sammy hasn't come to work today. He's called in sick." Miss Lawler looked worried. "I hope he—he's all right."

"What about Hoppy?" Trixie asked. "Did they find him?"

Nervously Miss Lawler fingered the golden chain around her neck. "There was no sign of the weather vane anywhere," she said. "It's disappeared."

Trixie drew a long breath. "Somebody has stolen Hoppy!" she exclaimed finally.

A Stranger in Town Hall • 8

STOLEN HOPPY?" Di's eyes widened. "Who would do a thing like that?"

Honey was speechless.

Mart scoffed. "Nobody from Sleepyside would steal Hoppy," he said. "Somebody probably just picked him up and hasn't turned him in yet."

"Hoppy's a valuable antique," Trixie reminded him. "A few years ago, someone stole the weather vane from Faneuil Hall in Boston, and I think—"

"Trixie," Miss Lawler snapped, her mouth tight with disapproval, "you have no right to make such an accusation. You're jumping to conclusions, and someone could be badly hurt by your thoughtless words."

Trixie's face grew red. "I—I—didn't mean—" she faltered.

"It's best to think before you speak, Trixie," Miss Lawler said. She turned and walked away.

"Wow!" Mart watched the teacher's aide hurry from the lunchroom. "What's she getting so uptight about?"

"I never saw her lose her cool like that before," Dan said.

The bell ending the lunch hour rang, and students began leaving the lunchroom. The Bob-Whites cleared off their table and headed for the door.

"I still think I'm right," Trixie said stubbornly. "We should go downtown right after school to tell Mr. Johnson and Sergeant Molinson."

"The sergeant isn't going to be happy to see you again so soon," Jim warned.

"I know," Trixie replied, "but he has to start looking for the thieves right away."

When school was over, the Bob-Whites wasted no time driving downtown.

There were several people standing around the common, including two police officers. Mr. Johnson, looking upset, was talking with the officers.

"Gleeps, the police are already working on it," Trixie said.

"That's a relief," Honey said with a sigh.

Seeing the officers head back to the station, Trixie waved to attract Mr. Johnson's attention. "Hi, Mr. Johnson," she called. "Any news?"

The caretaker shook his head. "Nothing, Trixie," he told her. "The weather vane is gone, and it's all my fault!"

"That's not true," Honey consoled him. "You couldn't do anything about the storm."

"That wind was pretty strong last night," Brian agreed.

But Mr. Johnson refused to be comforted. "No, it's my fault, all right," he insisted. "The base of the weather vane has needed fixing for a long time." Looking up at the cupola on top of the steeply pitched roof, he shook his head. "But that roof is pretty hard climbing for a man my age. I kept putting it off. To tell you the truth, I was going to have that new young helper of mine get to work on the base this week."

"You mean Sammy," Jim said.

"Yeah, Sammy," Mr. Johnson repeated. "He said he isn't afraid to climb. He probably could have fixed that base in no time." Wearily, Mr. Johnson rubbed his head. "Now it's too late," he said sadly.

Silently the Bob-Whites stared up at the high roof. The cupola looked oddly out of place without the handsome old weather vane in position.

"Well, I'd better get back to work," Mr. Johnson said. "I've got some papers on my desk that have to go to a roofing contractor this afternoon. I must have been up and down those stairs a dozen times already today."

"If you're tired, I'll go up and get them for you, Mr. Johnson," Trixie offered quickly. "Just tell me what to look for."

Mr. Johnson told Trixie where to find the papers, and she was off, running across the common to the front door of Town Hall. "See you at the car in a minute or two," Trixie called back to the other Bob-Whites.

The heavy front door closed solidly behind Trixie, cutting off the traffic noises from outside as suddenly

100

as turning off a radio. Inside, Town Hall seemed as quiet as a ghost town.

The two main meeting rooms on either side of the hallway were deserted. The long corridor that ran past the stairway was dark and gloomy-looking, and the stillness of the old building made Trixie feel she should walk softly. She went up the steep flight of stairs almost on tiptoe.

Mr. Johnson's office was at the far end of the second-floor corridor. The door was standing open. Trixie saw the folded papers on the desk where Mr. Johnson had said they would be. Tucking them into her jacket pocket, she started back down the hallway toward the stairs.

She had almost reached the stairs when she saw a door directly across from the stairway open slowly. A tall man backed out into the hall and soundlessly closed the door. Turning, he saw Trixie.

"Are you, uh, looking for someone?" Trixie asked, suddenly nervous.

"I'm looking for the caretaker's office," the man answered in an unfriendly tone.

"Oh." Trixie forced herself to smile. "That's it down there, at the end of the hall, but Mr. Johnson isn't in now. He's outside—"

"Thanks," the man interrupted. He turned and started down the stairs.

"Mr. Johnson is right out in the common," Trixie said helpfully.

"I'll talk to him later," the man called back, already at the bottom of the stairs.

"Jeepers!" Trixie scratched her head. "I wonder who that was." She turned to look at the closed door through which the man had come. The door was unmarked.

Twisting the knob, Trixie opened the door and poked her head inside. The small square room was dirty and completely empty, except for a narrow steel ladder bolted to the floor in the middle of the room. The ladder went up to a hatch set in the high ceiling.

Curious, Trixie started to climb, counting each rung as she went. After thirteen rungs, her head was pressed against the hatch. Hooking one arm around the top rung, Trixie cautiously pushed the hatch open. She smelled fresh air.

"This is the belfry!" Trixie exclaimed aloud. She stretched her neck to look around the empty tower, noticing the worn wooden floor, the low arched openings, and the weathered ceiling with another

102

hatch that led up into the cupola. "It isn't much bigger than Bobby's tree house," Trixie muttered. Then she gasped. "And come to think of it, I think that man was the same one I saw from the tree house!"

Bad News • 9

TRIXIE FOUND the other Bob-Whites waiting impatiently in the station wagon.

"Where have you been?" Mart demanded. "Clambering capriciously in the cupola?"

"As a matter of fact," Trixie said, sliding in beside him, "I *was* almost in the cupola. I climbed up to the belfry to have a look around."

"What!" Brian exclaimed.

"Trixie!" Honey gasped. "How did you—"

"On the ladder," Trixie said casually. "After the man asked me where Mr. Johnson's office was."

"Wait a minute, now," Jim ordered. He turned the station wagon onto the street and headed toward Crabapple Farm. "Okay, Trixie," he said, "how about starting at the beginning?"

Trixie told about seeing the man come out of the second-floor room. "He said he was looking for Mr. Johnson's office, and I told him that Mr. Johnson was standing right outside the building," she said. "There wasn't any sign on the door where he came out, so I just sort of looked inside."

"And?" Brian prompted.

"There wasn't anything in the room except a ladder up to the ceiling," Trixie said.

"And so you climbed it," Mart deduced. "Real smart. If the only thing in the room had been an open window, would you have defenestrated yourself?"

"De-what-a-strated?" Trixie asked.

"I think he means jumped out," Brian offered.

"Oh," Trixie said. "No, silly," she told Mart. "I was just curious about where the ladder went, since that man had just come out of the room."

"And the ladder went up to the belfry," Jim said.

"That's right," Trixie confirmed. "So, what was that man doing up there?"

"Elementary, my dear Beatrix," Mart said. "Mr. Johnson said he had some papers for a roofing contractor. That was the contractor, up looking at the roof. Case closed."

"Mart's right," Honey agreed.

"I'm not so sure," Trixie muttered.

Brian glanced at his watch. "We won't have time for our meeting now," he said gloomily. "But I guess it doesn't matter. With Hoppy gone, there's no reason to have a walk-a-thon. So we won't be on the radio, after all."

"At least for the time being," Trixie said with forced cheerfulness. "We can all hope that Hoppy will be found soon. If he is found, he could be recoppered before they put him back up on top of Town Hall."

"*If* he's found," Brian repeated as Jim pulled into the driveway at Crabapple Farm.

When Trixie, Brian, and Mart entered the kitchen, Bobby was singing "Meet me in St. Loooey, Looey" in a high, squeaky voice.

Brian and Mart were headed for the hall to hang up their jackets, and Trixie took hers off and handed it to Mart. "I'm sorry we're late again, Moms," she said.

"Meet me at the FAIRRR," Bobby sang at the top

of his lungs as he placed napkins at each place around the table.

"Who taught Bobby that old song?" Trixie asked.

Mrs. Belden smiled wanly. "The radio," she sighed. "WSTH has played it several times today. Someone has been calling in and requesting it." She rubbed her forehead and frowned. "Regan wants Bobby to exercise Mr. Pony tomorrow," she said, "and his school reopens the day after that, thank goodness. I've had a headache all day."

"You go and sit down, Moms," Trixie urged, feeling more guilty than ever about being late. "I'll finish getting dinner." Trixie picked up a spoon and took over at the stove.

"Hi, Trixie!" Bobby said, waving a napkin at her. "I know 'nother old-fashioned song now. Want to hear me sing it?"

"I believe I heard you singing when I came in," Trixie told him. Taking the silverware from the drawer, she handed it to her little brother. "Let's see how quietly you can put these on the table, Bobby," she whispered. "Moms has a headache."

Bobby made a silent O with his lips. "Okay," he whispered back. Tiptoeing to the table, he began his new task, very carefully placing each piece of silverware in its proper position.

Reddy began barking a minute later, and Bobby forgot to be quiet. "Here comes Dad!" he yelled. He and Reddy raced for the front door.

In spite of his avowed preference for hamburgers, Mart ate baked ham, scalloped potatoes, and buttered carrots with great enthusiasm. "It's delicious, Moms," he said. "Dinner fit for a despot."

"It wasn't cooked in a pot," Bobby objected. "It was cooked in the oven!"

"No thanks to me," Trixie said with a grin, then turned to speak to her father. "We stopped by Town Hall after school, Dad," she told her father.

"Oh?" Peter Belden buttered a hot roll. "Have they found the weather vane yet?" he asked.

"Not a sign of it," Brian answered.

"I'm sure it must have been stolen," Trixie said seriously.

Her father raised an eyebrow. "Stolen?"

Trixie nodded. "If the wind just blew Hoppy off the roof, someone would have found him by now. The wind surely wasn't strong enough to blow him very far away from Town Hall."

"That's true," her father agreed. "But why would anyone steal a weather vane, Trixie?"

"That weather vane is an antique," Mrs. Belden

108

pointed out. "It might be worth quite a bit of money. But I don't think that anyone in Sleepyside would steal it. Maybe it was just broken to pieces when it fell."

"There were no pieces found, either," Trixie persisted. "Hoppy just vanished."

Trixie and her brothers were cleaning up the kitchen after dinner when Mr. Belden yelled for them to come to the living room in a hurry. Wiping her hands on a dish towel, Trixie followed her brothers. The radio in the living room was on, and Trixie's father gestured for them to pay attention to what the announcer was saying.

". . . and the weather vane, made in the shape of a grasshopper, has been missing all day. The weather vane was apparently blown down by the storm, but the area around Town Hall has been searched thoroughly, and no trace of it has been found.

"The weather vane is about three feet long and weighs sixty pounds. It is over two hundred years old and believed to be one of the grasshopper vanes made by Shem Drowne, a Colonial coppersmith who crafted the famous grasshopper for Faneuil Hall in Boston. Authorities consider the Sleepyside weather vane to be very valuable, and it's feared that it has been stolen."

"There!" Trixie gasped. "See what I mean?"

Her father hushed her.

". . . a word from Sergeant Molinson of the Sleepyside Police," the newscaster continued.

"Good evening." Sergeant Molinson's familiar gruff voice came from the radio. "We must now assume that the antique weather vane from the top of our Town Hall has been stolen. The police department asks that all citizens of Sleepyside be on the alert. Any information concerning the possible whereabouts of the weather vane should be reported to the police at once. Thank you for your cooperation."

"Well, now it's official," Trixie said.

"You were right, young lady," her father conceded. "You know, it's funny—I must have looked at that weather vane a million times over the years, and I never gave a thought to the possibility that it might be valuable."

"I never did either," Mrs. Belden agreed. "Maybe it should have been on display in the museum, locked up in a case. But it's always seemed so—so natural for it to be up there on top of Town Hall."

Trixie slumped in a chair. "And we were going to announce our walk-a-thon on WSTH tomorrow," she said.

"Yeah," Brian added, "but there's no sense in trying to raise the money for recoppering the weather vane now."

"I hate to say this, Trixie," Mart mumbled. "But I think Hoppy's luck just ran out."

Bob-Whites on the Air · 10

HONEY TELEPHONED early the next morning. "Don't take the bus this morning, Trixie," she said excitedly. "Jim and I will come by for all of you in the station wagon."

"Okay," Trixie said. "What's up?"

"I don't have time to tell you now," Honey said. "See you in a few minutes."

Trixie told her brothers that Jim would be driving them to school.

"How come?" Mart inquired.

"I don't know," Trixie said, "but Honey was excited about something. I guess she'll tell us on the way to school."

Bobby stood with them near the back door as they waited for the station wagon. "I kinda wish I could go to school today," he said.

"What? Are these poor ears deceiving me?" Mart said. "A Belden who *wants* to go to school?"

"It's Tuesday," Bobby explained. "That's chocolate milk day. We get chocolate milk after recess in the morning."

Trixie mussed his hair. "I'm sure Moms will let you have some chocolate milk here after you get back from riding Mr. Pony," she said.

"Oh, yeah, Trixie," Bobby said with a smile. He waved her close and whispered in her ear: "Regan and me are gonna ride to my tree house."

"That's a good idea," Trixie whispered back. "You can tell me all about it this afternoon."

Jim honked, and Trixie and her brothers called good-bye to their parents and went out the door.

"Hi, everybody," Trixie greeted as they climbed into the station wagon. "What's going on, Honey?"

"Let me guess," Mart said. "Jim is lucubrating to become a bus driver."

"Not that I know of," Jim said.

"Wait till you hear!" Honey commanded happily.

"We're waiting," Brian urged.

"Well," Honey began, "last night I telephoned Mr. Perkins. I told him we were canceling our walk-a-thon, since Hoppy is missing, and that we wouldn't be making the announcement on his radio station."

"And?" Trixie prodded.

"And Mr. Perkins told me that he wants us to make *another* announcement for him, instead. He's going to offer a reward of one thousand dollars for Hoppy's return, and he wants us to announce it!"

"One thousand dollars!" Brian said.

"Wow!" Mart exclaimed.

"Why didn't you call and tell us last night?" Trixie asked.

"I promised Mr. Perkins I wouldn't say anything until this morning," Honey said. "The police asked him to wait for twenty-four hours before offering a reward."

"One thousand dollars," Trixie breathed. "That's a lot of money."

"Enough to keep me supplied with hamburgers for a year," Mart rhapsodized.

"Hey!" Trixie gasped. "If *we* found Hoppy, then we could donate the reward to have him recoppered."

"That's fine," Brian said. "But where do we start looking for him?"

"I don't know," Trixie admitted. "When are we going to make the announcement, Honey?"

"We're supposed to be at the station right after school," Honey said. "Mr. Perkins said we could rehearse for a while, and then tape the announcement when we're ready. It'll be on the evening news."

"The evening news," echoed Mart with satisfaction. "I always did want to be an anchor person."

That afternoon, the Bob-Whites made their way to the reception room at WSTH. The radio station was housed in a new brick and glass building on the outskirts of Sleepyside.

Stepping to the receptionist's desk, Honey introduced herself. "I'm Honey Wheeler, and these are my friends—"

"Oh, yes." The attractive young woman smiled. "Mr. Perkins is expecting you. Come with me, please."

As the receptionist stood, the phone rang and a switchboard light blinked. She punched a button and picked up the receiver. "Station WSTH," she said. "May we play a song for you?" She listened for a moment, then said, "Yes, sir. We're always happy to play a request."

115

When she hung up, the young woman shook her head. "That's the fifth time today that same man has called to request the same old song. He must be crazy about 'St. Louis Blues.' Come with me. I'll show you to the recording room."

She led the Bob-Whites down a short corridor and into a small, nearly empty room. A single row of chairs lined one wall, and a microphone stood in the middle of the floor.

"You'll use this room to record your announcement," the receptionist told them. "It seems a bit small, but we don't usually have seven people at a time making recordings." She pointed toward a window in one wall. "The disc jockey and the engineer are in there," she said. "Make yourselves comfortable. Mr. Perkins will be with you in just a minute."

After the receptionist had gone, Trixie looked around the room. "This isn't what I thought the inside of a radio station would be like," she said in a disappointed tone.

"What did you expect?" Jim asked. "Tubes and wires and transistors all over the place?"

"My parents love this station," Di said. "They listen to it a lot."

Trixie nodded. "Moms says the old songs really make her feel good."

"Except when Bobby sings them," Mart added wryly.

The door opened then, and Mr. Perkins came into the room. He was a small man with snow-white hair and a neatly clipped moustache. He looked every bit as dignified as a wealthy and successful man should, but his smile was warm and friendly while he shook hands with each of the Bob-Whites as Honey introduced them.

"Thank you for coming," Mr. Perkins said. "I understand that you young people are rather well known in the community for being helpful to those in need. Well, this business of the weather vane being stolen has me upset. I haven't lived in Sleepyside for too many years, but I know that the grasshopper weather vane is an important part of the town's history.

"Your plan to raise money with a walk-a-thon and have the weather vane recoppered was a splendid idea. It showed that you are proud of Sleepyside's heritage. But now, we must direct our efforts toward getting the weather vane back. I can't think of anyone I'd rather have announce the reward I'm offering for the return of the weather vane."

Mr. Perkins handed each of the Bob-Whites a sheet of paper. "I wrote seven short paragraphs," he told them, "so that you can take turns reading. Each one

117

of you can read one paragraph."

Dan glanced at the sheet and nodded. "We can each take a turn. We'll do it in alphabetical order."

"Fine, fine," Mr. Perkins said. "Go through it a few times, and let me know when you're ready to record. I'll be in the next room there with the engineer. You can signal me through the window."

The Bob-Whites watched as Mr. Perkins adjusted the microphone to the proper height. "Now, don't be nervous. If we have to, we can record this a dozen times, but I'm sure you'll get it right on the first try."

Those words of encouragement gave Trixie and the others the confidence they needed. Silently, each of them read over the script.

"Okay," Brian said, "let's run through it now. I'll go first."

Brian stepped to the microphone and began. "Where is our weather vane? The copper grasshopper has been missing from the Town Hall roof since Sunday night."

Dan followed. "The weather vane had been standing on Town Hall for over two hundred years—ever since Sleepyside was founded."

Di was next. "The grasshopper is three feet long and weighs sixty pounds. It has round glass eyes, and its body is hollow. A long, thin spire passes through

118

its body to hold it on its base."

Honey spoke up. "Sleepyside's weather vane looks very much like the famous grasshopper atop Faneuil Hall in Boston. Some people believe that Shem Drowne, the coppersmith who created the Boston weather vane, also made one for Sleepyside."

Jim continued. "The weather vane may be a valuable antique, but more important, it is a meaningful part of Sleepyside history."

Mart went on. "Raymond Perkins, owner of this radio station, is offering a reward of one thousand dollars for the return of the weather vane."

Trixie's turn had come. "Any information about the weather vane or the person or persons responsible for its theft should be given to the police department or to Mr. Perkins at station WSTH."

Then, with great feeling, Trixie added, "Please, everybody who's listening—help us find our Sleepyside weather vane."

Mart looked up, surprised. "Hey, that isn't in the script."

A little embarrassed, Trixie shrugged. "It just popped out," she said. "Do you think it would be okay to say it on the recording?"

"Indeed it would," Mr. Perkins said, entering the room. "I listened through the speaker in the next room," he confessed. "You all sounded like professionals! Let's record."

The Bob-Whites were still glowing with pride when they crowded into Wimpy's for colas on the way home.

"Our elocution certainly sounded effective," Mart said.

"Let's just hope it helps to get Hoppy back," Trixie added.

Bobby Takes a Tumble • 11

As THE BOB-WHITES SIPPED their colas, Trixie grew unusually quiet.

"Now what are you ratiocinating about so intently?" Mart asked.

"I'm *thinking*—about Hoppy, of course," Trixie replied. "Suppose the wind didn't blow him off the roof of Town Hall. Is there a way that someone could have taken him down?"

"I've kind of wondered about that myself," Jim

admitted. "If somebody actually planned to steal Hoppy, they wouldn't wait around for a storm to blow him down. They'd figure out a way to go up and get him."

"Hey, that's right," Mart said.

"How would anybody get Hoppy down from the roof?" Di asked.

"A ladder?" Honey offered.

"I don't think so," Trixie said, shaking her head. "Where would anybody get a ladder that tall? The only ones I've ever seen that could get that high are the ones on a fire engine."

"Maybe we ought to look on the roof of the fire department and see if they have a new weather vane," Brian joked halfheartedly.

"How about a crane?" Dan put in.

"No," Mart said. "Too heavy. A crane would have left deep tire marks in the grass on the common."

Honey nodded. "And besides, somebody would have noticed a big thing like that."

"Nobody was outside that night, though," Trixie reminded her. "And the power was off, so there weren't any lights."

"Let's drive by the common and see if we come up with anything else," Mart suggested.

"That's a good idea," Trixie said. "I'm ready; let's

122

go!" She sprang to her feet.

A few minutes later, Jim pulled the station wagon into the parking lot not far from the common. The offices in Town Hall were closed, and the building was dark inside. The big elm trees behind the building had lost most of their leaves, and the empty cupola on the roof was especially noticeable against the late afternoon sky.

"I wonder—" Trixie began.

"Hey!" Honey interrupted. "There's Sammy. He must be feeling better now."

Sammy was cutting across the common, walking with his hands in his pockets and eyes downward. He reached the sidewalk and passed the station wagon without looking up.

Mart rolled down the window and called, "Hey, Sammy!"

The young man jumped and looked almost as if he were going to run. When he recognized the Bob-Whites, a look of relief came over his face. "Oh, it's you," he said.

"I didn't mean to startle you," Mart apologized.

As Sammy came up beside the station wagon, he pulled a small white earphone from his ear and patted the transistor radio in his shirt pocket. "I was listening to music. I didn't hear you drive up." He ran his

123

fingers through his hair. "I just finished working, and I'm beat."

"Maybe you shouldn't be working so hard, Sammy," Honey said, "if you've been sick. And it must have been awfully busy around here today."

Sammy glanced up at the empty cupola. "The whole deal is a mess," he snapped. "I almost wish I'd never come to this place."

Trixie couldn't help but feel sorry for him. "You really are tired," she said. "Can we give you a lift somewhere? We're on our way home from WSTH—"

"That hick station?" Sammy interrupted scornfully. "What were you doing there—helping them dust off all their moldy oldies?"

Honey flushed. "Mr. Perkins, the man who owns the station, is a good friend of my parents," she said softly.

"That's their problem," Sammy said.

Trixie was upset now. "Mr. Perkins is a very nice person. He's putting up the re—"

"Aw, I'm only kidding," Sammy said. "I'm sorry. I really am tired. My truck's just up the street. See you guys later." He pushed the earphone back into his ear and walked off, whistling a familiar-sounding tune.

"I never expected Sammy to act like that," Di said, surprised. "I wonder what's wrong with him?"

124

"He's just tired," Dan said. "Everybody gets cranky once in a while."

Brian shook his head. "Sammy seems kind of odd at times," he said. "I can't quite figure him out. He's almost like two different people."

"Know what?" Trixie spoke up. "Sammy lied to us. He told me and Honey that he was a 'rock music freak.' But I think he's listening to WSTH right now, and they're playing old-fashioned music."

Jim turned on the radio in the station wagon, already tuned to WSTH. The melody playing was the same one that Sammy had been whistling.

"See?" Trixie said. "What's that tune?"

"I'm not sure," Jim said. "But it isn't rock music."

"Try to remember the tune," Brian prompted. "We'll ask Moms what it is when we get home."

"Speaking of getting home," Jim said, "that's what we'd better be doing." He started up the engine, looked over his shoulder, and pulled the station wagon back onto the street.

A few minutes later, Jim dropped Trixie and her brothers off at Crabapple Farm.

"Hey, everybody, come and look at me," Bobby called from upstairs when he heard the door open. "I'm a invalid!"

"Jeepers!" Trixie hurried up the stairs, with Mart and Brian right behind her.

Bobby was propped up in his bed, wrapped in a blanket. One of his eyes was bruised and swollen almost shut, and he wore two bandages on the side of his face. He grinned, enjoying the opportunity to surprise the big kids.

Mrs. Belden was sitting in a chair beside the bed. "Bobby could hardly wait for you to get home and see his bruises," she said with a shake of her head.

"Bobby!" Trixie exclaimed. "What in the world happened to you?"

Brian touched the skin around his little brother's eye with gentle fingers. He whistled softly. "Wow! That's quite a black eye you've got there," he said.

"Yup," Bobby agreed. "Mr. Pony got scared and runned away—and he tossed me off just like that!" Bobby tried to snap his fingers but gave up. "I didn't cry, though," he boasted. "I just got up and caught Mr. Pony, the way you did, Trixie, when he got scared before."

Trixie gently mussed her small brother's tousled curls. "Good for you," she praised.

Mrs. Belden stood. "Stay here and talk with him while I go put his dinner on a tray," she told Trixie and her brothers.

Trixie sat down beside Bobby. "Tell us all about it," she urged.

"Well—" Bobby drew a long breath—"Mr. Pony and I were riding along near my tree house," he began, forgetting to keep his secret from the boys. "Regan was there, too, but he was working over by that old road. All of a sudden, the wind blowed real hard, and a big pile of leaves went flying all around—" he waved his hands in an arc—"and . . . and a big critter scared Mr. Pony! Mr. Pony went '*EEEEE-eeee!*' and jumped up in the air, and I fell off."

"Wow," Trixie said. "Did it hurt?"

"Yeah!" Bobby's eyes clouded with a hint of tears, which he blinked back. "But I was worried about Mr. Pony, so I chased him, and I caught him! I talked to him, like you did, Trixie, till he wasn't scared anymore. Then I took him over to Regan. Regan washed all my cuts and put on these bandages and brought me home to Moms. He told her he was real proud of me."

Trixie smiled. "I'm proud of you, too, Bobby," she said. "And I'm sure glad you aren't badly hurt."

"Moms says I have to go downtown to the doctor tomorrow before I go back to school," Bobby declared, feeling very important. "That's to make sure I'm not broken. And then," he added, beaming with delight, "Moms says we can get hamburgers at Wimpy's, just like you big kids do."

Brian laughed. "You're getting to be a 'big kid' yourself," he said.

"Moms said she'd bring the radio up here so I can hear you on the radio tonight," Bobby announced. "Are you gonna sing?"

Trixie fluffed his pillow and tucked his blanket around him. "No, silly," she said. "We're going to talk about Hoppy, remember? I'll go down and help Moms with your dinner now, okay?"

"Don't forget the chocolate milk," Bobby reminded her.

Down in the kitchen, Trixie helped her mother prepare a tray with Bobby's dinner.

"How did the announcement turn out?" Mrs. Belden asked.

"We were all pretty nervous at first," Trixie admitted. "But Mr. Perkins is so nice, he made it seem easy."

Mrs. Belden poured chocolate milk into Bobby's glass. "I'm sure you all did a great job," she said.

"I just hope someone will be able to collect that reward soon," Trixie said. "Everyone has been watching for anything suspicious, but Hoppy may already be a long way from Sleepyside."

"Maybe your announcement on the radio will help to track him down," Mrs. Belden said.

"That reminds me," Trixie spoke up. "What's the name of this tune, Moms?" She whistled the tune that Sammy had been whistling in front of Town Hall.

"You must have picked that up at WSTH," Mrs. Belden said, shaking her head. "They've been playing it all day. It's 'St. Louis Blues.'"

Trixie Finds a Clue · 12

RIDING THE BUS to school the following morning, Trixie told the others about Bobby's accident.

Mart nodded. "He has a fuliginous oculus," he said with a smirk.

Di gasped. "That sounds terrible!"

Brian smiled. "I think Mart's talking about a black eye," he said.

Honey looked relieved. "Bobby was lucky. Being

thrown from a horse, even a pony, can sometimes be serious."

"Moms is taking him to the doctor this morning for a checkup," Trixie told her.

"Speaking of mothers," Honey said, "my mother's birthday is this week. I'm going to go shopping for her gift after school. Do you and Di want to come with me?" she asked Trixie.

"Sure," Trixie agreed at once.

Di shook her head. "I can't. I have a piano lesson this afternoon."

"That beats chopping firewood," Dan said with a grin. "I'll be busy after school for weeks."

The bus pulled into the parking lot, and the young people gathered their books and headed for their homerooms.

Before the bell rang, Trixie opened her notebook to look one last time at her social studies report. "Gleeps!" she yelped. "I forgot my report!"

"Oh, no," Honey said. "Are you sure?"

Trixie searched through an untidy collection of classroom notes. "It's not here," she said with a doleful sigh.

"Miss Craven doesn't like late reports," Honey cautioned.

"Quoth the Craven, 'Nevermore!'" Mart chimed in quickly.

Trixie glared at Mart, then turned back to Honey. "You're right, Honey," she moaned. "I'll call Moms and ask her to drop my paper off at lunchtime. She'll be in town with Bobby."

Trixie hurried to the pay phone at the end of the hall and called her mother.

"You're just lucky I was going to be in town," her mother scolded gently. "Don't worry, though. Bobby and I will drop your paper off at lunchtime."

"Thanks, Moms!" Trixie said. "See you then." She hung up and sighed with relief.

Morning classes passed quickly, and before Trixie knew it, it was time for lunch. Trixie chatted with the other Bob-Whites and munched on her chicken sandwich until she saw Bobby's curly head poking around the lunchroom doorway.

"Over here, Bobby," Trixie called, waving to her little brother.

"Hi, everybody!" Bobby said after racing across the room ahead of his mother. "Trixie, I'm not broken anyplace—and I found something new for my coin collection! Look at this!"

Bobby held out a blackened coin. "I found it when

I wasn't even lookin'," he said, "and Moms says that makes it a good-luck piece!"

Brian took the coin and examined it. "This is an old silver dollar," he said, surprised. "Where did he find this, Moms?"

"On the common," Mrs. Belden answered, handing Trixie her social studies report. "We were crossing the green to the parking lot after leaving the doctor's office."

Jim took the coin and rubbed it with his fingers. "I can't make out the date," he said, "but this coin looks pretty old to me."

Trixie jumped up, excited. "Let's go show it to Miss Lawler!" she suggested. "She knows all about coins."

Mrs. Belden glanced at her watch. "Do you have time, Trixie?" she asked.

"Sure," Trixie said, already crossing the room with Bobby beside her. "We've got ten minutes before the bell. And besides, I want you to meet Miss Lawler. You'll like her."

Holding Bobby's hand, Trixie led the way to the social studies classroom.

Miss Lawler was sitting alone at her desk, reading as she ate her lunch. The classroom door was open, and Trixie called, "Are you busy, Miss Lawler? I'd like to introduce you to my mother and my brother Bobby."

"Come in, Trixie." With a friendly smile, the teacher's aide stood to shake hands. "Mrs. Belden—Bobby, I'm happy to meet you," she said.

Mrs. Belden smiled warmly. "Trixie and the boys have talked a lot about you," she said. "They all enjoy this class."

Bobby fidgeted. "Want to see somethin'?" he asked. He thrust his hand out, showing the coin. "I found it today."

"My goodness, Bobby," Miss Lawler said, taking the coin from him and looking at it carefully. "This is a Seated Liberty silver dollar. I can't quite read the date, but I can tell you that it's at least one hundred years old."

"Wow!" Brian exclaimed. "That's quite a find!"

"It certainly is," Miss Lawler said, handing the coin back to Bobby. "Take good care of it," she told him.

Bobby pushed the coin down deep into his pocket. "I'm going to put it in my collection," he said.

Miss Lawler smiled. "Do you have a coin collection, like Mr. Quinn?" she asked, pointing to the display case beside her desk.

134

Bobby shook his head. "Nope," he answered. "I collect *everything*. Moms says it's junk, but Trixie thinks it's good stuff, don't you, Trixie?"

Trixie poked her little brother in the ribs, making him giggle. "Sure I do," she said. "Uh-oh, there goes the bell."

Brian and Mart waved and left at once. Mrs. Belden took Bobby's hand. "That means it's time for us to go to Wimpy's," she told him. "Miss Lawler, do drive out and see us soon," she urged. "It's only two miles to Crabapple Farm."

"I—I'd really like to, but I don't drive," Miss Lawler said softly.

"Then we'll drive in and get you," Mrs. Belden offered. "Your brother Sammy is welcome to come, too."

Miss Lawler's face paled, and she turned away quickly. "I—I don't have a brother," she murmured softly.

The others were amazed. "We all thought Sammy was your brother," Trixie explained. "He calls you Sis—"

"That's short for Cecilia, my first name," the teacher's aide said, tidying her desk. "Sammy is just— a friend."

135

"Gleeps. I'm sorry," Trixie apologized.

"That's all right," Miss Lawler said. "You'd better hurry to your class. It was nice to meet you, Mrs. Belden, Bobby."

When Trixie entered the social studies classroom for the last period of the day, she placed her report neatly on her desk and winked at Honey.

Honey smiled and winked back. Miss Craven was a popular teacher, but she wouldn't tolerate late papers without a good excuse. "I forgot" was *not* a good excuse.

The class was almost over before Miss Craven mentioned that the reports were due. "Please leave your reports with Miss Lawler on your way out of the room," she said, standing up behind her desk. She walked toward the door, adding, "Good afternoon, class." Her timing was perfect—the bell rang just as she reached the door.

The students talked and laughed as they walked up the aisles and handed their papers to the teacher's aide. Honey and Trixie were the last ones in line.

"Thank you," Miss Lawler said automatically, adding their papers to the pile. She looked worn out and pale.

"Are you feeling all right, Miss Lawler?" Honey asked in her kind way.

The teacher's aide managed a faint smile. "I'm worried . . . about Sammy," she murmured. "I haven't heard from him since he told Mr. Johnson that he was sick. I just hope he's okay."

"Oh, he's fine," Trixie assured her. "We saw him last night. He'd been working late."

"Really?" Miss Lawler looked relieved. "That's good to hear. I think I'll wait here for him. Sometimes he drops by when he's finished at Town Hall." She took one of the reports from the pile. "I have plenty to keep me busy," she added.

"We'll see you tomorrow," Trixie said.

Outside, Trixie and Honey buttoned their jackets and went down the walk headed for town. They walked briskly, enjoying the feel of the sharp October air on their faces.

"I'm kind of glad Di couldn't come," Trixie admitted. "This gives us time to do some serious thinking about Hoppy."

"We always do think best when the two of us are together," Honey agreed.

"That's why the Belden-Wheeler Detective Agency

137

will be successful," Trixie said seriously. "We're a good team, Honey. But we goofed with Hoppy," she went on. "When we didn't see him on the ground that morning after the storm, we should have known right away that someone had taken him."

"But what could we do?" Honey asked.

Trixie shrugged. "I still wish I could figure out if there was a way to steal the weather vane from the top of the cupola," she said.

Honey frowned. "Me, too. Someone would have to be able to fly in order to—"

"Honey! That's it!" Trixie exclaimed. "A helicopter! That's what they used to steal Hoppy. It would be easy for a helicopter to hover over the roof and hook the weather vane with a rope."

"I don't know . . ." Honey began hesitantly.

"And what's more," Trixie rushed on, "we *saw* the helicopter! Remember the night we were showing Hoppy to Miss Lawler and that helicopter came down so low?"

"But Hoppy wasn't stolen that night," Honey objected.

"Of course not," Trixie said. "They couldn't steal Hoppy while we were there watching them. They were casing Town Hall!"

138

"They were *what?*" Honey asked.

"Casing the job—looking it over and making plans." Trixie was flushed with excitement. "Then, when the lights were out on the night of the storm, they came back and stole the weather vane."

Trixie started to run ahead. "We've got to get to the police station and tell Sergeant Molinson about this," she called.

Honey was not as anxious to visit the burly police officer. He didn't appreciate Trixie and Honey becoming involved in police matters and did not hesitate to tell them so. "Maybe we should wait," Honey said. "We don't really know—" But Trixie was already too far ahead to hear. Honey sighed and ran to catch up.

When they reached the police station, Trixie hurried inside and headed for the sergeant's desk. "We have important information for you, Sergeant Molinson," she said breathlessly. "We know how the weather vane was stolen!"

Sergeant Molinson scowled. "Let me guess. A giant gorilla climbed up the side of Town Hall and—"

"I'm serious," Trixie interrupted. "I should have realized it sooner, but Honey and I actually *saw* the thieves."

Sergeant Molinson's jaw dropped. "You *saw* some-one steal the weather vane?" he demanded.

"No," Trixie corrected. "We saw them casing the job—from a helicopter!" Trixie went on to tell the sergeant how she and the other Bob-Whites had seen the helicopter hovering over Town Hall.

The sergeant looked skeptical, but he listened carefully.

"It was the Saturday before last," Trixie concluded, "between nine and ten o'clock, right after the first show at the theater let out."

Sergeant Molinson wrote down the information. He fidgeted with his pencil for a moment, thinking, and then asked, "What was the weather like that night?"

"It was beautiful," Honey said. "The sky was clear, and there was a big moon, and—"

"And how about the weather on the night the weather vane was stolen?" the sergeant interrupted curtly.

"That was the night of the big storm," Trixie said. "The wind was blowing so hard that—that. . . ." She paused. "Gleeps. Could a helicopter fly in all that wind?"

Sergeant Molinson rubbed the back of his neck. "I

don't know," he admitted. "But I'll check into it."

As Trixie and Honey turned to leave, Sergeant Molinson grumbled, "Thanks for the information, anyway. It's more than I've had to go on so far."

Miss Lawler and the Stranger • 13

AFTER LEAVING the police station, Trixie and Honey went to a popular gift shop nearby to shop for Mrs. Wheeler's birthday gift.

Honey had no trouble choosing presents—a beautiful scarf and a delicate china figurine. "Mother loves figurines," Honey declared, "and this one is absolutely perfect."

While the presents were being wrapped, Honey called for a cab. It was waiting for them when they came out of the shop a few minutes later with the packages in their arms.

Honey gave directions when they were seated. "Crabapple Farm on Glen Road, please, and then up to Manor House."

The cab started with a jerk, knocking Honey sideways against Trixie.

"Good driver," Trixie whispered.

"Good and fast," Honey replied.

The cab lurched to a halt at the stoplight in front of the school building. "I can hardly wait to take driver training," Trixie said. "No more depending on someone else to drive me around."

Honey nodded. "Then we can take turns driving the Bob-White station wagon. That will be lots of fun."

Glancing out at the school building, Trixie was surprised to see someone coming out the front door. "I didn't think anyone would still be in the building this late," she said.

"Probably just the janitor," Honey guessed without much interest.

"No, it's Miss Lawler," Trixie declared. "And there's a man walking up the path to meet her, but it isn't Sammy."

"Really?" Honey leaned over to watch.

On the walk in front of the school building, Miss Lawler shook hands with a tall man and then walked with him to his car parked by the curb. As the man held the car door open for the teacher's aide, Trixie recognized him with a start.

"Jeepers!" she gasped. "That's the man who was in the belfry at Town Hall! And—and that's the same car that I saw following you that night outside Wimpy's."

"Are you sure?" Honey asked nervously.

Trixie nodded. "I'm sure. Honey, there *is* something strange about that man. And there's some kind of connection between him and Miss Lawler. It's obvious that she knows him."

"It could be he's a friend of Sammy's," Honey suggested as the light changed and the cab pulled ahead.

"I didn't know Sammy had any other friends in Sleepyside," Trixie said uncertainly. "I think something is going on . . . and I wish I could figure out what it is."

"Ah, here's the dilatory detective now," Mart said to Trixie when she came into the kitchen a few minutes later. "Get hung up on the way home?" he inquired.

144

Trixie took off her jacket and tossed it to Mart. "Thanks for offering to hang up my jacket," she said. "I'm going to go change into my jeans, Moms, and then I'll be right down to help."

Mrs. Belden was taking a casserole from the oven. "Everything's just about ready, Trixie," she said. "Call Dad and the boys when you come back downstairs."

While they ate, Trixie told about visiting the police station. "I told Sergeant Molinson about that helicopter we saw. He said he'd get to work and investigate it immediately."

"I can't imagine why you didn't think of it before this," Mrs. Belden said. "It certainly does sound suspicious."

"We'll see if they mention it on the news after dinner," Mr. Belden said.

Trixie and her brothers hurried to clean up the dishes after dinner and entered the living room just in time to hear the end of the local weather forecast on WSTH.

"And now for more news," the announcer said. "Today, for the first time since the theft of the weather vane from Sleepyside's Town Hall, the police department received what sounded like a promising new lead. Young people reported seeing a helicopter

145

hovering over the Town Hall the week before the weather vane was stolen."

Trixie held her breath and listened intently to the newscast.

"However," the newscaster continued, "the helicopter seen that night was found to belong to the National Guard Training Camp. Student pilots were being trained in night flying. There are still no clues to the whereabouts of Sleepyside's missing weather vane."

Mr. Belden snapped off the radio, and Trixie sagged with disappointment.

"So much for that idea," Brian said. "Too bad, Trix. I thought your idea about the helicopter sounded pretty good."

"Don't worry, Trixie," Bobby tried to comfort her. "You and Honey are real good 'tectives. You'll find Hoppy."

Trixie shook her head. "Maybe. If we're lucky," she said in a dismal voice.

"Here, Trixie," Bobby said. "You can have this." He handed her a rusty metal button. "It's a new good-luck piece I found today."

Trixie smiled. "Thanks, Bobby," she said. Tucking the button into her pocket, she headed upstairs to do her homework.

146

As she tried to work a math problem, Trixie's mind buzzed with questions. *If they didn't use a helicopter, how did they get Hoppy off that roof?* she wondered. *Maybe they* did *use a giant gorilla!*

A Shocking Discovery • 14

WHEN THE BOB-WHITES entered Sleepyside Junior-Senior High the next morning, they saw a commotion in the hallway outside the social studies classroom. Students and teachers were crowded around the doorway, which was blocked by a burly policeman.

"Jeepers! What's going on?" Trixie wondered aloud.

"I hope no one is sick or hurt," Honey said.

"Let's go find out," Trixie urged, heading for Miss

Craven's classroom. The others were right behind her.

The police officer held them back at the doorway. "No one is allowed in this room at the moment," he said.

"There's Trixie," Miss Lawler said from inside the room. "She and Honey drew the pictures I told you about."

Sergeant Molinson called to the officer at the door. "Let Trixie and her friends come in."

The policeman stepped aside.

As soon as the Bob-Whites stepped into the room, they saw Mr. Quinn's display case tipped over on the floor. The glass had been smashed, and the case was empty.

"The coin collection is gone!" Trixie gasped.

Miss Lawler, chalk-white and trembling, sat at her desk. Miss Craven, distraught-looking and dabbing at her eyes with a handkerchief, nodded to Trixie.

"It's a terrible, terrible thing," Miss Craven said sadly. "I never thought anything like this could happen in our school. I saw a light in this room last night as I drove past, and I'll never forgive myself for not stopping to investigate."

Trixie's eyes met Honey's. Both knew they were sharing the same thought.

Sergeant Molinson opened his notebook. "What time did you drive past the school and see the light, Miss Craven?"

Trixie stiffened, dreading the answer.

"I'm not sure, exactly," Miss Craven said. "I didn't look at my watch. But I believe it was around four, or perhaps a little after four."

Honey gasped.

"Oh, no," Trixie murmured.

"What's the matter?" Di asked softly.

Trixie cupped a hand around her mouth and whispered, "I'll tell you later."

"Did you see anyone around the building, Miss Craven?" the sergeant asked, making notes in his book.

"No, I didn't," Miss Craven said. "Just the light in the classroom."

Sergeant Molinson nodded and turned to Miss Lawler. "Now, how about you, Miss Lawler?" he asked the teacher's aide. "Can you tell us anything at all?"

"No," Miss Lawler answered without looking up. "I—I stayed for a short while after the class had finished, but—"

"Why did you stay?" Sergeant Molinson asked quickly.

"Well, I had some papers to gather up," Miss Lawler said.

Trixie frowned. *She doesn't want to get Sammy involved in this,* she thought. *I wonder if he showed up after Honey and I left.*

"I didn't see anyone in the building as I left," Miss Lawler concluded.

"What time was that?" the sergeant asked.

"Just at four o'clock," Miss Lawler answered in a firm voice. "I'm certain of the time, because I—I had an appointment at four."

Sergeant Molinson closed his notebook and turned to Trixie and Honey. "Miss Lawler is going to lend your reports to us so we can make copies of the coins you drew. Mr. Quinn is out of town, but those papers will give us something to go on. I hope your drawings were accurate."

Trixie and Honey nodded.

"That's all, then," the sergeant said. "I'll be in touch," he told Miss Craven.

For the rest of the morning, Trixie found it impossible to concentrate on her classes. She was uptight and bewildered by the mysterious theft of the valuable coins.

When Trixie and Honey entered the social studies

classroom that afternoon, Miss Craven's eyes were still red and swollen.

"Miss Lawler will not talk about the coins this afternoon," Miss Craven said softly. "By now you are all aware that the coin collection was stolen last night. Instead, we'll begin immediately with today's lesson."

At the end of the period, Trixie and Honey waited while the other students left the room. They carried their books up the aisle to Miss Lawler's desk, and Trixie said, "Miss Lawler, we're—"

Before they reached her desk, Miss Lawler picked up her papers and stood. "I don't have time to talk," she said. She turned abruptly and hurried from the room.

Honey looked hurt.

"She's avoiding us," Trixie said softly.

As the Bob-Whites rode home from school, Trixie suggested a special meeting for the following afternoon, when she knew all of them would be able to come. "We've got two mysteries on our hands now," she said. "And Honey and I have a few things we think you all should know about."

After school on Friday, all seven members gathered at the clubhouse. After Jim called the meeting to order, Trixie took over.

"Honey and I saw something the night before last on the way home from town," she said. She went on to tell about seeing Miss Lawler and the stranger from the belfry shaking hands in front of the school building.

"It was around four o'clock," Honey added. "About the time Miss Craven said she saw the lights on in the social studies room. And we know that Miss Lawler planned to stay late—she told us she was going to wait for Sammy."

Trixie nodded slowly. "But I guess she was really waiting for that stranger. It looks like she helped him steal the coins," she said sadly. "They must be partners in crime."

"Oh, no!" Di protested. "I don't believe it! Miss Lawler wouldn't steal the coins!"

"Why didn't you tell this to Sergeant Molinson yesterday?" Jim asked.

"Because he didn't ask me," Trixie said, flushing. "I wanted to talk about it with the rest of you Bob-Whites first."

"Maybe that man is Miss Lawler's boyfriend," Dan suggested.

Trixie shook her head. "They didn't greet each other like friends. It seemed more like a—a business meeting," she said.

Mart pointed a quick finger at Trixie. "Was Miss Lawler carrying a package or anything?" he asked sharply.

Trixie stopped to think. "No," she answered. "But she was carrying that big tote bag she always carries."

Jim groaned. "I've seen that bag," he said. "She could carry *ten* coin collections in it."

Unhappy and frustrated, Trixie pushed her hair back from her hot forehead. "It sure looks like Miss Lawler and that stranger are working together. We all know that Miss Lawler is a new-newmis—"

"A numismatist," Mart put in.

"Right," Trixie continued. "She would know if the coins were valuable. She'd know where to sell them, too."

"I'm afraid you may be right," Jim said.

"Are you going to tell Sergeant Molinson?" Di asked.

Trixie sighed. "We'll have to tell him what we saw," she said. "We don't have any real proof that Miss Lawler was involved, thank goodness. I guess Honey and I will have to stop at the station on Monday after school."

When the meeting was over, everyone was gloomy and quiet. There was none of the chatter and laughter that usually followed their get-togethers.

"It doesn't look very good for Miss Lawler," Brian said as he locked the clubhouse door.

"Well," Trixie said as the Bob-Whites started home, "at least Moms will be happy today—I'll be home in time to help with dinner." She brightened and turned to the others. "Why don't all of you come and have dinner with us? It'll cheer us up. Moms is baking beans and brown bread, and our bean pot is *huge*. There'll be plenty for everybody."

Mart's gloom lifted a little. "Yeah—and we can add spheroids of spicy chopped meat encased in delicate skin—"

Trixie giggled. "He means cut-up hot dogs," she explained. "Mart has trouble with little words like that."

"It sounds good anyway," Jim said. "Your mother makes the best baked beans this side of heaven, Trixie. How about it, Honey, shall we accept this dinner invitation?"

"Let's," Honey answered quickly. "Mother and Dad are in New York, and I'm sure Miss Trask won't mind. I'll call her from Trixie's."

"How about you, Di? Dan?" Brian asked.

"Sorry. I'm out," Dan said. "I'm still cutting firewood. Mr. Maypenny can't handle that anymore."

Di looked disappointed. "I promised Mother I'd

155

help with the twins," she said. "But thanks anyway."

"Maybe next time," Trixie said.

"Don't worry," Brian added. "Mart'll eat extra helpings in your names!"

Surprising News • 15

In the backyard at Crabapple Farm, Bobby was playing with Reddy, the Beldens' big Irish setter. Trixie and the others had cut through the orchard, and Brian signaled them to a halt in the shadows where they could watch without being seen.

"Pay 'tention, Reddy," Bobby said. "This is how you roll over." Bobby rolled over in the leaves that covered the lawn. "See? Now you do it. Roll over!"

Reddy wagged his tail and licked Bobby's face.

"No, no! Don't *kiss!* Roll over!" Bobby rolled over once more. "Like that, see?"

Trixie and the others burst out laughing. "Who is training whom?" Mart asked as they all emerged from the shadows.

"Hi, everybody!" Bobby shouted. "I teached Reddy a neat trick. Watch!" He picked up a large stick and threw it with all his might. "Go fetch, Reddy!" he ordered.

The big dog bounded across the yard after the stick. Trixie and Honey exchanged glances—Reddy was not famous for his discipline.

"Pay 'tention," Bobby urged. "Reddy's a smart dog; you'll see."

Reddy came bounding back with the stick in his mouth. He dropped it at Trixie's feet.

"Good boy, Reddy!" Bobby said, patting the dog vigorously.

Brian shook his head. "That wasn't right, Bobby," he said. "Reddy should have brought the stick back to you."

Bobby shrugged. "Why? I don't want it."

This brought more laughter.

Looking at Honey and Jim, Bobby brightened. "Oh, Honey and Jim, are you going to stay for dinner?"

Brian poked Bobby in the ribs, making him squeal

with delight. "You bet they are," he said.

Jim and Honey followed the Belden young people into the kitchen. "We couldn't help it, Mrs. Belden," Jim said in mock apology. "Trixie and the boys forced us to come for dinner."

"Good! We like company," Mrs. Belden said. She was very fond of Honey and Jim and treated them as if they were her own children. "As long as you're here," she suggested, "why not spend the night?"

"That's super, Moms!" Trixie exclaimed. "Honey and I both have dental appointments in the morning. We'll go together."

"And we'll do some work on my car," Brian, already making plans, said to Jim.

Bobby clapped his hands. "Stay! Stay!" he shouted.

Honey laughed. "We thought you'd never ask," she said. "Of course we'll stay."

"Terrific," Trixie said. "Now tell us what we can do to help, Moms."

"Well," Mrs. Belden said, "the boys can bring in some firewood. We'll pop corn after dinner."

"Oh, boy!" Bobby whooped, heading for the living room. "I'll go fix the pillows on the floor right now."

"And, Trixie," Mrs. Belden continued, "we're all out of hot mustard. Would you and Honey go down to Mr. Lytell's for a jar?"

"That's a long walk, Moms," Brian said quickly. "Jim can drive them down in my car, if he can get it started. Mart and I will bring in the wood."

"Thanks, Brian!" Trixie and Honey chorused.

A few minutes later, Jim, Honey, and Trixie were rattling down Glen Road in Brian's old jalopy. "It's not a limousine," Trixie said, "but it's better than walking!"

At Mr. Lytell's small country store, they parked in front and hurried inside. They were the only customers there, and Mr. Lytell was getting ready to close for the day.

"A jar of hot mustard, please," Trixie ordered.

Mr. Lytell placed the mustard on the counter and waited for Trixie to fish coins from her pocket. "Having a big dinner party?" he asked, eyeing Honey and Jim.

"No, just the family," Trixie answered the inquisitive storekeeper. Honey and Jim exchanged amused glances.

"I see that young fella with the yella truck is back in town," Mr. Lytell said as he counted out the change. "I saw you and Honey riding with him the other day."

"I think you're mistaken, sir," Honey said politely. "Sammy is new in Sleepyside."

160

"Can't tell me that!" Mr. Lytell snapped. "That yella truck was up and down here all summer long, drag racing on the old Louis Road. And that young fella and his roughneck friends were in this place lots of times."

Trixie looked at Honey and Jim and shrugged. "If you say so, Mr. Lytell," she said. She picked up the jar of mustard and opened the door. "Good night, Mr. Lytell. Thanks."

"Do you think it really was Sammy?" Honey asked when they were back in the jalopy.

"I doubt it," Jim said. "Mr. Lytell might have seen that old truck, though. Sammy may have bought it from someone around here."

As Jim started to back out onto the road, Honey warned, "Hold it, Jim; there's a car coming."

"It's coming pretty fast, too," Trixie added. "It looks like a big station wagon."

Jim looked over his shoulder to watch the approaching car. As the big wagon passed the lighted storefront, the young people had a glimpse of the driver and passenger.

"I think that's Miss Lawler and Sammy!" Honey exclaimed.

"And Miss Lawler was driving," Trixie observed. "She said she couldn't drive!"

"Miss Lawler looked like she was scared," Honey pointed out.

Jim turned onto the road. "Sammy's probably teaching her to drive," he said. "Glen Road is good for beginners—you don't meet many other cars here. Everybody's a little scared when they first start driving. You and Trixie'll find that out."

They were almost home when another car came down Glen Road toward them. "Gleeps," Trixie said. "Glen Road is turning into a regular freeway!"

Jim chuckled as the car went by. "Glen Road isn't private, Trix," he said. "Anybody can use it." He signaled and turned into the driveway at Crabapple Farm. "I hope those beans are ready."

Everyone agreed that the dinner of brown bread, baked beans, and frankfurters was delicious. Mrs. Belden's huge bean pot was scraped clean, and not a crumb of brown bread remained.

When they had finished eating, the young people ordered Mr. and Mrs. Belden out of the kitchen. "Go sit in the living room and relax by the fireplace," Trixie said. "We'll be in as soon as we clean up the dishes."

Trixie and Honey filled the sink with soapy water while the boys cleared the table. Everyone helped dry and put away dishes and silverware.

The boys were already in the living room, and Honey was hanging up her towel, when Bobby came bursting into the kitchen.

"Trixie, I almost forgot," he said. "I found a lot of neat things in the woods today. You and Honey can wash them for me, please." He dropped a fistful of things on the counter. "Thanks!" he added, running back to the living room.

"Here we go again," Honey said with a smile, taking the towel down from the hook.

Trixie spread Bobby's newest possessions out on the counter. "More lucky stones," she groaned. "Two white ones, one black, and one brown this time. And jeepers! Another old baseball card!"

Gingerly, Trixie pushed the muddy card aside, revealing a small round piece of metal under it.

"What's that?" Honey asked, peering over Trixie's shoulder.

"Some kind of coin, I think," Trixie said, picking it up. She washed it quickly and took a closer look. "Honey! This is a Chinese coin! See the writing?"

"Let me see," Honey said, bending to look.

As they studied the coin, Trixie's face paled. "Honey, this might be one of Mr. Quinn's coins! We'd better ask Bobby where he found this."

"Wait, Trixie," Honey said quickly. "We're not *sure* this coin is from the stolen collection. Let's not get everybody excited until we can find out."

"How'll we do that?" Trixie asked. "Mr. Quinn is out of town."

"The library is right across from the medical building," Honey pointed out. "We can stop there after we're done at the dentist."

"You're right," Trixie said, drying off the coin and putting it in her pocket. "I think they have Mr. Quinn's papers on his coin collection. We'll check and see if this coin is mentioned."

They washed Bobby's lucky stones, and Trixie dropped them all into the bottom drawer of the cabinet. "The 'junk drawer,'" she told Honey.

"Don't forget the card," Honey said.

"Ugh. Can't wash that." Trixie grimaced and dropped the dirty card into the drawer with the stones. "Let's go see what everybody else is up to," she urged, heading for the living room.

The Beldens and their guests sprawled on the floor in front of the fireplace, talking and laughing and listening to music on WSTH. Mart convinced his mother to demonstrate her ability with tongue twisters for Jim and Honey, and soon all the young people were convulsed with giggles.

After a while, Mr. Belden brought out the old-fashioned corn popper, and everyone took turns shaking it over the glowing embers. As they munched on the tasty hot popcorn, the music from the radio stopped abruptly.

"We interrupt this program for a word from our news department," the announcer said.

Everyone stopped talking and turned to listen.

"The valuable antique weather vane, thought stolen from the roof of Sleepyside's Town Hall, has been found."

Trixie jumped up. Honey gasped.

"A young man, recently employed as assistant caretaker—"

Trixie said excitedly, "He means Sammy!"

"—discovered the weather vane in a small room directly beneath the belfry of Town Hall. The weather vane, shaped like a grasshopper, was wrapped in canvas and apparently undamaged. Station manager and owner Raymond Perkins will be presenting the assistant caretaker with a check for one thousand dollars tomorrow. We'll have more details on the morning news. Now, back to our music."

"That's impossible!" Trixie exclaimed, jumping to her feet. "I was *in* that room on the day after Hoppy was stolen, and it was completely empty! If Sammy found Hoppy in that room, then somebody had to put him there later."

"Are you absolutely certain the room was empty?" Brian prompted.

"Positive!" Trixie insisted.

"Wow," Mart breathed. "It looks like Hoppy's a phantom weather vane!"

The Stranger Appears Again • 16

TRIXIE WAS OUT OF BED, bending and touching her
toes, when Honey opened her eyes the next morning.

"Do you always wake up so full of pep?" Honey
asked, yawning.

Trixie laughed. "It's just nervous energy," she said.
"I'm excited about Hoppy and nervous about going
to the dentist."

Honey giggled.

"I'm going to wear the same jeans I wore yester-day," Trixie said. "They feel good and comfortable now. You'll find clean tops in the second drawer."

The girls dressed quickly and went down to the kitchen for breakfast. Brian, Mart, and Jim were already at the table, helping themselves to scrambled eggs.

Trixie hurried through breakfast, impatient to get downtown. "We have a lot to do this morning," she told the boys.

Jim grinned and looked at Honey. "I guess it's a good thing I went up to Manor House this morning and brought over your bike," he said. "It's outside with Trixie's."

"Thanks, Jim!" Honey said, delighted. "I'm so glad we adopted you," she added.

"Don't forget to brush your denticles," Mart reminded the girls.

A few minutes later, Trixie and Honey were pedaling down Glen Road as fast as they could. They reached town in record time.

The girls stopped at the medical building and put their bikes in the bike rack.

Honey looked over at the common, diagonally

across the street. "It'll sure be good to have Hoppy back up there on Town Hall," she said.

"Look, there's Sammy," Trixie said. "Let's go over and congratulate him."

They hurried across the street and onto the grass of the common. "Congratulations, Sammy!" Trixie called.

"We heard the great news on the radio last night," Honey told him. "You must feel pretty good!"

"Like a million bucks," Sammy bragged. "A thousand, anyway."

"Did you get the reward money already?" Honey asked.

"Naw," Sammy grumbled. "Old man Perkins wants to have some kind of ceremony when he presents the check."

"That's a nice idea," Trixie said.

Sammy scowled. "I wish he'd just give me the money. I earned it—I should get it now."

Trixie changed the subject. "We saw you last night."

Sammy looked alarmed. "Oh, is that so? When? Where?"

"Riding with Miss Lawler in a big station wagon," Trixie said. "On Glen Road."

"Were you teaching Miss Lawler to drive?" Honey asked.

"Teaching Cis? That's a laugh. She's known how to drive for a looong time," Sammy said. "That station wagon belongs to her."

Trixie and Honey exchanged glances. Honey began to say something, but Trixie motioned her to stop.

"I have to get to work," Sammy said. "I don't like to work on Saturdays, but I've got a lot of stuff to do."

"Are you going to repair Hoppy's base?" Trixie asked.

"Yeah," Sammy said. "I'll fix it up real good."

Trixie glanced up at the cupola. "How do you get up there?"

"Why do you care?" Sammy queried.

"I was just wondering," Trixie said. "It's too tall for a ladder. Is there any way to get up there from outside the building?"

Sammy eyed her curiously for a moment. "Nope," he answered. "Only way up there is from inside the building. There's a room with a ladder that—"

"I know," Trixie interrupted. "I guess that means whoever stole Hoppy got up there from inside the building."

170

"The building was locked," Sammy said abruptly. He looked directly into Trixie's eyes. "And I don't have the keys," he added in a menacing tone.

Honey coughed self-consciously. "I—I can't wait to see Hoppy," she said.

Sammy's face brightened. "You want to see Hoppy? Follow me!" He swaggered off, heading for the front door of Town Hall.

Honey pulled Trixie back. "Let's not," she said. "Sammy makes me feel creepy today. Besides, we don't want to be late for the dentist."

"We have lots of time," Trixie insisted. She ran to catch up with Sammy. "How did you ever find Hoppy?" she asked as they went inside the building.

Sammy laughed. "It was easy. I just looked in the right place," he bragged.

Trixie and Honey followed him up the stairs and into the small room with the ladder.

The room was dim and dusty, just as Trixie remembered, but now it wasn't empty. A large canvas-wrapped bundle stood in one corner.

Sammy lifted a portion of the dirty canvas, and Trixie and Honey saw the copper face of the big grasshopper, with two green glass eyes staring straight at them.

171

"Oh!" Honey gasped. "I didn't realize Hoppy was so big."

"Hello, Hoppy," Trixie said softly. She bent to touch the old weather vane.

Instantly Sammy dropped the canvas back over the weather vane. "Keep your hands off it!" he warned.

"I wasn't going to hurt Hoppy," Trixie said, flushing. She took a deep breath to calm herself and surveyed the room. "I still can't understand it," she said, puzzled. "I was in this room right after Hoppy was stolen, and it was *empty*. Somebody must have carried Hoppy into Town Hall and put him in this room."

"I don't know about that," Sammy said with a shrug. "But right here's where I found it, and that Perkins guy didn't say anything about where it had to be to collect the reward. Easiest thousand bucks I ever made."

"I'll bet it is," Trixie muttered to herself. She glanced at her wristwatch. "Honey and I have to go now," she said. "We've got appointments with the dentist."

"See ya around," Sammy called as they went down the stairs.

As they were crossing the common, Trixie glanced over her shoulder to make sure no one was near. "Sammy is lying," she said to Honey.

"What do you mean?" Honey asked.

"He couldn't have just found Hoppy sitting there in that room," Trixie declared. "I think he *put* Hoppy there himself."

"But, Trixie, that would mean—"

"I know what it would mean. It would mean that Sammy stole the weather vane. And when he heard about the reward, he brought it back and pretended to find it in that room."

"But how could Sammy steal the weather vane?" Honey asked. "You heard him say that there's no way to get up on the roof except from inside the building."

"I know," Trixie admitted. "I haven't figured that part out yet."

The girls entered the dental clinic and registered with the receptionist. Trixie was called almost immediately. An examination revealed no cavities, and a quick cleaning was all she needed. Honey was called next.

Half an hour later, they were on their way out the door.

"We must use the right toothpaste," Trixie said.

173

Honey nodded. "Now we'll have plenty of time for the library," she said.

The public library was on the edge of the common, directly across from the medical building. Comfortable and delightfully old-fashioned, the big white building was originally one of the first homes in Sleepyside. Now it made a perfect place for reading.

The librarian was busy at her desk when Trixie and Honey entered the main reading room.

Trixie spoke softly to her. "Could you help us?"

The librarian looked up and smiled. "I'll try," she said.

Trixie reached into her pocket and took out the coin Bobby had given her to wash. "We'd like to see any information you have on Mr. Quinn's coin collection," she said. "We need to know if he has a coin like this."

The librarian took a look at the coin. "Oh, no," she said. "Mr. Quinn's Oriental coins are all Chinese. This is a Japanese yen. Mr. Quinn doesn't collect Japanese coins at all."

Trixie shrugged. "I guess that's that," she said, hiding her disappointment. "Thanks anyway."

"But that is a coincidence," the librarian murmured. "I believe a Japanese yen was one of the artifacts placed inside the weather vane."

"What?" Trixie asked. "We know Hoppy is hollow, but we never knew there were things inside him."

"Oh, yes, indeed," the woman said, leaning forward with her arms on the desk. "That's another reason why the weather vane is so valuable. It's really a sort of time capsule of Sleepyside."

"Do you have a book about the artifacts?" Honey asked eagerly.

The librarian shook her head. "No. But we do have all the old newspaper clippings about the weather vane. They're all kept downstairs in the reference department."

Trixie and Honey exchanged glances. Both had the same idea. "Are we allowed in the reference room?" they asked in one voice.

The librarian laughed. "Of course," she said. "It's a bit gloomy down there, but you won't have any trouble finding the clippings about the weather vane. I had them out for Mr. Perkins a few days ago, and several people have been in looking at them since then. Look for a folder labeled 'Town Hall' on the shelf of newspaper clippings. The folders are in alphabetical order."

"Thank you. We'll find it," Trixie said happily.

Trixie and Honey went down the narrow steps to the basement and entered the reference room. It was crowded with rows of high metal shelves with narrow aisles between them. The newspaper clipping files were on the far side of the room.

Trixie located the Town Hall file and lifted it from the shelf. She and Honey began to sort through the faded brown clippings.

"Listen to this," Honey urged, reading aloud from a clipping that included a picture of the weather vane:

> "In 1878, the weather vane was taken down from Town Hall to be replated. At that time, a small copper cylinder, engraved with the words LUNCH FOR GRASSHOPPER, was placed inside the hollow body of the old vane. A number of artifacts were inside the cylinder. The artifacts included the front page of the evening paper, the business card of Mayor Davis, a silver dollar, a Japanese yen, an Indian head penny, and a Civil War button."

"Gleeps!" Trixie blurted. "Bobby found an old silver dollar on the common! He found an old metal button in the woods, too! A silver dollar, a button, and a Japanese yen," she said slowly. "They're all things that were inside Hoppy. Hoppy was hidden in the woods!"

176

Honey caught her breath. "Are you sure?" she asked.

"Positive," Trixie declared. "Remember when Bobby got thrown off Mr. Pony? He said Mr. Pony got scared by a 'big critter.' I'll bet that was Hoppy! The cylinder must have opened when he was moved, and some of the things inside fell out. Bobby found them near his tree house, so Hoppy must have been hidden somewhere around there."

"But why was he hidden?" Honey queried. "Why didn't the thief just take him out of town?"

Trixie pushed a hand through her curls, frowning. "I'm not sure," she said slowly. "Maybe the police alert scared him. Or maybe he expected a reward to be offered and was just waiting for that."

"We should tell Sergeant Molinson about the things Bobby found," Honey said.

"We will," Trixie agreed, "but first let's get Bobby to show us where he found them, and where he saw the 'big critter.' Then we can give them to Sergeant Molinson and tell him—"

"I'll take that Japanese coin," a man's voice said from behind them. "Hand it over, please."

Startled, Trixie and Honey whirled around. "The man from the bell tower!" Trixie gasped.

"Don't be frightened," the man said in an even tone. "Just give me the coin."

When Trixie didn't move, the man said, "All right . . ." and reached under his coat.

"No—don't—" Honey whimpered.

In a panic, Trixie threw the newspaper file in the man's face, releasing a flurry of old clippings. "Run, Honey!" she shouted.

Both girls dashed down the aisle and out of the room. They bounded up the stairs two at a time.

"In here!" Trixie said, pulling Honey into a closet at the top of the stairs.

Almost immediately they heard running footsteps coming up the stairs, past the closet, and going out the side door of the library.

After a moment, Trixie opened the closet door a crack and peeked out. Cautiously, she and Honey stepped from their hiding place.

"Did—did he have a gun?" Honey asked shakily.

Trixie managed a weak smile. "I didn't want to wait and find out," she said. "Don't mention this to anybody till we ask Bobby where he found those things. As soon as we get home, I'm going to look at that old card Bobby gave us last night. I'll bet it's Mayor Davis's business card."

Honey sighed. "All right," she said. "But if we go searching around in the woods, I want the boys to be with us."

"Right," Trixie agreed. "Let's go!"

Down in the Woods · 17

WHEN TRIXIE AND HONEY turned their bicycles into the driveway at Crabapple Farm, they found the boys at work on Brian's old jalopy.

"Ah, just in time for lunch," Mart said, wiping his hands on a greasy rag. "How did you fare the lancinations of the periodontal practitioner?"

"If you're asking about the dentist," Honey said, "we both did fine—no cavities."

"Never mind about that," Trixie blurted. "Wait till

you hear what we found out at the library." She told about the artifacts that had been placed inside the weather vane and about her suspicion that Sammy had stolen it and then returned it.

Brian raised his eyebrows. "Wow," he said softly. "Bobby found a real old silver dollar right on the common."

"And he also found an old metal button, a Japanese yen, and some kind of card," Trixie informed him, "somewhere in the woods."

"Let's go look at the card," Honey urged.

"Wait a minute," Trixie warned. "Let's not get Moms and Bobby all excited. I'll take a look at the card while Honey and I are helping Moms fix lunch. If it's the right one, I'll let you know."

"And then what?" Mart queried.

"Then we'll offer to take Bobby for a romp in the woods," Trixie said. "And we'll see if he can remember where he found those things."

"Good idea," Jim said. "Maybe we'll find some other clues out there."

The others agreed.

Half an hour later, Mrs. Belden called the boys in for lunch. "Be sure and get those hands clean before you set foot in the house," she warned.

As the young people took their places around the

table, Trixie gave a significant little nod to Brian, Mart, and Jim.

"I'll be having lunch downtown with your father," Mrs. Belden announced. "I'm going to go change clothes. Trixie, please see that Bobby eats all of his lunch."

"I will, Moms," Trixie assured her.

"Bobby," Mart said, passing the sandwich platter, "tell us about that 'big critter' that scared Mr. Pony in the woods."

"Well. . . ." Bobby munched on his sandwich. "It was a awful big huge a-nor-mous giant bug!" he said. "It had big round eyes, like this—" Bobby widened his eyes as far as he could—"and funny-looking legs." He made a face. "It was the ugliest bug I've ever seen. I was scared, too, just like Mr. Pony."

Trixie poured Bobby some more milk. "Do you remember where you saw the big bug, Bobby?" she asked.

"Sure," Bobby answered. "He was just a little bit away from my tree house, right beside the tire tracks."

"Tire tracks in the woods?" Mart queried.

"How'd you like to take us all down and show us?" Jim asked.

Bobby licked the mayonnaise from his fingers.

182

"Nope," he answered. "I can't. I'm going downtown with Moms. I get to go to the barber all by myself, while Moms has lunch with Dad." He helped himself to a cookie. "Trixie can find them for you. She knows where my tree house is, and those tire tracks go right by it to the old road."

"All ready, Bobby?" Mrs. Belden came back into the kitchen, dressed in a stylish pants suit. "We'll see you big kids later," she said. "If you're planning to go out later, take Reddy along with you. He needs some exercise."

"Okay, Moms," Trixie said. "Have a nice lunch." After the two were gone, she turned to the others and said, "Bobby never mentioned tire tracks before. Whoever hid the weather vane out there must have driven into the woods on that old road."

"Shall we go get the horses and ride out there?" Honey asked.

"No, it'll take too long to get them saddled up," Mart said hurriedly. "Besides, we'll have a better chance of coming across any new clues if we're on foot."

Brian was already opening the door. "Mart's right," he said. "Let's go! We'll walk down the old road and keep a lookout for tire tracks."

"That reminds me, Trix," Jim said as they left the

house. "Regan checked, and the 'Dead End' sign had been removed from the entrance to that road. Regan made a new one himself and put it up."

"Let's be sure to look and see that it's still there," Trixie said.

The young people walked briskly along Glen Road to the entrance of the old road that ran beside the woods. Reddy hurried along ahead, stopping frequently to wait for the others to catch up. Regan's hand-lettered sign, with a white background and red letters, was impossible to miss. " 'Louis Road—Dead End,' " Trixie read aloud, stopping by the signpost. "I never knew this road had a name," she added, surprised.

"Dad told me that this section of the woods was once owned by a family named Louis," Jim recalled as they walked down the road. "They were French. The name is actually pronounced *Looee,* but most people use the American version, *Lewis.*"

"Mr. Lytell said something about Louis Road the other night," Honey said, "but I didn't know what road he was talking about then."

Now that she knew where to look, Trixie had no trouble spotting Bobby's tree house, back away from the road.

When they reached the old ROAD ENDS sign, they

184

saw tire tracks leave the road and go off into the woods. "Here's just where I saw the bell tower man," Trixie said, standing at the end of the road.

"There are two different sets of tracks leaving the road," Brian pointed out. "Whoever hid the weather vane must have used two cars—one to bring it here, and another to take it back."

They followed the tire marks into the woods to a spot that was extra thick with leaves. The remains of what had been a wide, high pile of leaves were still visible.

"The wind didn't pile those leaves up like that," Trixie asserted. "Somebody raked them in to bury Hoppy."

Everyone bent down and scanned the ground for more clues. Reddy bounded around among them, his long ears flopping and his big feet sending the leaves flying. Finding a stick, he loped up to Trixie, wagging his tail and ready to play.

"Good boy, Reddy," Trixie said automatically. She was down on her knees, hunting close to the ground for clues.

Reddy pawed Trixie's arm insistently and dropped the stick beside her, demanding attention.

"Okay, Reddy, you win," Trixie said. She picked up the stick. "Jeepers!" she exclaimed. "This isn't a

185

stick—it's metal. It looks like it belongs to Hoppy somehow!"

The others crowded around to examine the weathered piece of metal Trixie held in her hand. Reddy pushed his wet nose between Jim and Brian, keeping an eye on his "stick."

"You're right," Brian said. "I think that's a piece of the spire from the weather vane."

"Here's what happened," Trixie conjectured quickly. "Sammy drove down here with Hoppy in the back of his old yellow truck and hid him under a pile of leaves. That was the 'critter' that frightened Mr. Pony."

Mart scratched his head. "Why didn't Sammy just get out of town with the weather vane right away?"

"I think I've figured that out now," Trixie said. "Hoppy would be in plain sight in the back of the pickup truck. Even wrapped in canvas, he wouldn't be too hard to recognize. I'll bet that Sammy had already arranged to hide Hoppy here and have a partner pick Hoppy up later."

"Sounds logical," Jim said. "But how would the partner have known when or where to come? They would have needed some sort of signal. . . ."

"Gleeps," Trixie said. "The radio!"

"Huh?" Mart questioned.

"The song," Trixie said, her face lighting up with the realization. "The signal to come and get Hoppy was a song played on WSTH—'Meet Me in St. Louis'! Moms said that someone requested that song over and over on the day after the storm, remember?"

Brian snapped his fingers. "That's it!" he exclaimed excitedly.

Trixie brushed her hair away from her forehead. "I didn't get the connection until just now," she admitted. "I never knew this was Louis Road until I saw Regan's sign."

"The bell tower man must be Sammy's partner," Honey guessed. "He was supposed to meet Sammy here and take Hoppy away in his car."

Jim looked thoughtful. "Then why *didn't* they take the weather vane and leave?" he asked.

Trixie pondered. "I'll bet they decided it would be easier to take Hoppy back and collect the reward than to try to get him out of town."

Brian looked smug. "And there was another signal," he said, "for Sammy to tell his partner that their plans were changed."

The others looked at him, bewildered.

Brian smiled. "Remember when we went to WSTH to announce the reward?" he asked. "The receptionist said someone kept calling and requesting the same song over and over again that day."

"'St. Louis Blues'!" Honey exclaimed. "Brian, I'm sure you're right!"

Jim nodded toward the piece of metal in Trixie's hand. "With that and the other things Bobby found, we have proof that the weather vane was hidden here. But we still don't have any proof of Sammy's involvement."

"Yipes," Trixie said, suddenly turning pale. "I just had a terrible thought."

"What's that?" Jim asked.

"Well," Trixie said, "if we assume that Sammy stole Hoppy, and that the bell tower man is Sammy's partner, then that involves Miss Lawler, too."

Honey gasped. "You're right, Trixie. Because we saw Miss Lawler and the bell tower man together—and it looked like they knew each other."

Brian shrugged. "That would mean that the three of them are partners," he said.

"And," Mart added, "they probably stole Mr. Quinn's coin collection, too. It all fits."

"It sure looks like it," Trixie admitted sadly. "But Jim is right—we don't have any way to *prove* that any of them are involved."

"We do have a lot of things that should be turned over to Sergeant Molinson, right away," Jim pointed out. "I suggest we head for Manor House, get the station wagon, and go to town right now."

"We need to get Mayor Davis's card, too," Trixie remembered. "Let's go back to Crabapple Farm. We can go to town in Brian's jalopy . . . assuming it's still running after you worked on it this morning."

"It's running better than ever," Brian assured her. "Let's go!"

Mrs. Belden and Bobby were not yet back when the young people filed into the kitchen half an hour later.

"I'll leave a note for Moms," Trixie said, "telling her that we went into town."

"We may be a while," Jim cautioned.

"I'll tell Moms we'll get dinner at Wimpy's," Trixie added. "That'll save her some trouble at dinner time tonight."

A few minutes later, they were crowded in Brian's jalopy, chugging down Glen Road toward town. Trixie carried the broken spire and the other artifacts in a small grocery sack on her lap.

Halfway there, Brian's jalopy coughed and sputtered and coasted to a stop. The boys jumped out and pushed the car to the side of the road, then opened the hood and peered inside.

Trixie, still in her seat, bit her lip and tried to stop the thought that kept going through her head. *We may be sending Miss Lawler to prison,* she thought. *She* can't *be Sammy's partner . . . can she?*

A Squirrel Gives a Clue • 18

TRIXIE SAT in the backseat of Brian's stalled jalopy and fidgeted with the sack in her lap.

"We'll have it going again in no time," Brian called from behind the raised hood. "I think."

Trixie turned to Honey. "I'm too nervous to just sit," she said. "Let's get out and walk. The boys can catch up when they get the car going again."

"Okay," Honey agreed.

They told the boys that they were going to walk

on ahead, and in a few minutes, the jalopy was out of sight behind them.

"What's bothering you, Trixie?" Honey asked as they walked down Glen Road.

Trixie scowled. "I just can't believe that Miss Lawler is a thief. I'm *sure* that Sammy stole Hoppy, and I'm pretty sure that the bell tower man is Sammy's partner. But Miss Lawler knows both of them, and she was responsible for Mr. Quinn's coin collection—"

"And the coin collection got stolen, too," Honey completed.

"Right," Trixie said. "So if we prove that Sammy stole Hoppy, and he gets arrested . . . then Miss Lawler will probably end up in jail, too."

"But we can't prove that Sammy stole Hoppy," Honey reminded her. "All we can prove is that Hoppy was hidden in the woods."

"That's the other thing that's bothering me," Trixie said. "There must be a way to prove that Sammy stole Hoppy. I just can't figure out what it is."

Trixie and Honey glanced over their shoulders from time to time, but there was no sign of Brian's jalopy. Before long, they were on the outskirts of town.

Honey giggled. "I guess we should have taken the

station wagon after all," she said.

Trixie nodded and looked at her watch. "I don't know whether we should go to Sergeant Molinson right now or wait for the boys."

"Let's sit and rest a minute," Honey suggested, pointing to one of the benches that were placed around the edge of the common.

The girls plopped down on the bench and looked around. The common was deserted, and the late afternoon light cast eerie shadows through the bare tree branches.

Honey shivered and turned the collar of her jacket up. "It looks kind of spooky," she said.

Trixie pointed to a fat squirrel crossing the common. "He doesn't look too scared," she said with a grin.

As the girls watched, the squirrel stopped to sit up and nibble on something it found on the dry grass. When it was through eating, it looked around, sniffing the air, and then scampered off toward Town Hall.

"He must live in one of those trees," Honey said, pointing to the stately old elms that stood along the back of the building.

Trixie's eyes widened, and her mouth dropped wide open.

"What's the matter, Trixie?" Honey asked in a concerned tone.

Trixie pointed, and Honey watched as the squirrel started up the side of one of the trees. The animal climbed quickly, then hurried along a big horizontal branch. At the end of the branch, the squirrel paused for a moment, then jumped—and landed on the roof of Town Hall!

"That's it!" Trixie exclaimed. "That's how Sammy got up on the roof!" She stood up and ran toward the tree.

"Wait, Trixie," Honey called, running to catch up.

Trixie stopped at the base of the tree and looked up. The first branch was several feet off the ground, but there were lots of branches spaced close together above it.

"Perfect for climbing," Trixie said.

"If you're a squirrel," Honey said breathlessly.

Trixie put her sack down. "Give me a boost," she said.

Honey gasped. "Trixie! You're not going to—"

"I'll just climb up a little way and see how it looks," Trixie said.

"But you might fall," Honey wailed.

Trixie shook her head. "I'll be careful. I used to be the best tree-climber in Sleepyside, back in my old tomboy days. Come on, give me a boost."

Reluctantly, Honey struggled to boost Trixie up to the first branch.

"A little more . . ." Trixie urged. "Just a little— there!"

Trixie pulled and scrambled and got herself up onto the branch. The next branches were easy. "Just like climbing a ladder," she called down to Honey.

"That's high enough, Trixie," Honey called back. "Please come down!"

"Just a little farther," Trixie said. "I'm almost there." She reached the big branch that hung out over the roof of Town Hall, straddled it like a horse, and paused to catch her breath. For the first time, she looked down.

"Yipes! I guess it is a little higher than it looks," she said.

"What?" Honey yelled. "I can't hear you."

"No problem," Trixie called, trying to sound more confident than she felt. Very carefully, an inch at a time, she began to slide herself along the branch toward the roof.

"Trixie! Come down!" Honey pleaded.

As Trixie inched forward, the branch began to bend under her weight, and in a minute, the end of the branch was touching the roof of Town Hall.

Trixie kept her eyes straight ahead and forced herself to keep going.

Suddenly she was there. Trixie eased herself off the branch and straddled the steeply pitched roof.

As soon as her weight was off the branch, it snapped back to its original position—just out of reach above Trixie's head.

Uh-oh! Trixie thought. *Now what do I do?* She couldn't see Honey anymore, and it was rapidly growing dark. The belfry, with the cupola on top, was about twenty feet ahead.

"Honey, can you hear me?" she called.

"Yes," came Honey's voice from below. "Are you all right?"

"I'm fine," Trixie said a little shakily. "But I can't reach the tree branch to get back down."

"Oh, Trixie! I'll go and get Sergeant Molinson."

"No, wait," Trixie called. "I can get in the belfry and climb down the ladder into the building. I think I can unlock the front door from inside."

"Trixie! Let me go get help!"

"Just wait a minute," Trixie shouted. "I'm sure I can make it." She began to slide herself along the peak of the roof toward the belfry. She was almost there when something shiny caught her eye. It was a small disk of metal caught in one of the shingles

196

below her, reflecting the last red rays of the setting sun.

Trixie leaned forward until her stomach touched the peak of the roof and very slowly and carefully reached downward. She stretched her arm to its limit, trying not to shift her weight and slip off the peak. Her fingertips touched the metal disk, and she slid it free from the shingle and retrieved it with a sigh. Sitting up once more, Trixie held her discovery up to the fading sunlight. It was Sammy's buffalo nickel!

"There's the proof," Trixie gasped. "This must have fallen out of Sammy's pocket when he climbed up here to steal Hoppy!"

She was only a few feet away from the belfry now. Every muscle in her body ached from the strain as she slid herself closer . . . closer. Finally, she was able to reach up and hook her hands over the edge of one of the tall, narrow openings that were spaced along the sides of the belfry. She pulled herself up, trying to gain a foothold on the slippery shingles. Struggling to hang on, she banged her knees against the belfry and scraped her ankles on the roof. When her stomach was even with the edge of the opening, Trixie pitched forward and toppled into the belfry. For a moment, she lay limp with exhaustion on the dirty floor, gasping and panting.

There was a large metal ring set in one end of the trapdoor in the floor of the belfry. Trixie stood and brushed herself off, then squatted in front of the ring and pulled with all her might. The heavy door creaked open, exposing the ladder that went down inside Town Hall.

Trixie took a deep breath and started down the ladder.

Danger! • 19

IN THE ROOM below the belfry, Trixie waited for her eyes to become accustomed to the darkness. She could make out the door off to one side, and, hands outstretched like a sleepwalker's, she headed for it. At the door, she groped along the wall beside the doorframe until she found the light switch. Her eyes burned from the sudden glare of the single bare bulb hanging from the ceiling.

In the opposite corner of the room, the canvas-wrapped bundle was still leaning against the wall. Trixie walked to it and lifted a corner of the canvas, exposing the large copper head of the grasshopper weather vane. Gently, Trixie patted the head. "Hello, Hoppy," she said quietly.

She lifted more of the canvas and discovered a small leather bag close to the weather vane. Dropping to her knees, Trixie picked up the bag. It jingled with the sound of coins! With trembling fingers, Trixie pulled the bag open and looked inside. She recognized the coins immediately.

"Mr. Quinn's coin collection—it's all right here!" she exclaimed. At the same moment, she heard footsteps in the hallway outside!

"Somebody's coming this way," she gasped.

Dropping the bag of coins beside the weather vane, Trixie dashed across the room and turned off the light. Finding her way back to the steel ladder, she climbed quickly, but couldn't make it all the way up before the door opened.

Miss Lawler and Sammy came into the room.

Sammy carried a flashlight in one hand and a gun gripped tightly in the other. The gun was pointed at Miss Lawler!

"Aw, stop your bawling," Sammy said roughly. "By the time anybody notices that broken window downstairs, we'll be long gone."

"Sammy," Miss Lawler said in a pleading tone, "you've been doing so well since you left the halfway house. Everyone was proud of you. You've got a job now, and you can go to college next year . . . you've got a good life ahead of you."

Sammy's laugh was harsh and scornful. "Who needs college?" he said. "I'd rather make my money the easy way. And this time I won't get caught, either."

"Sammy," Miss Lawler said, "you've got your thousand dollars now. Just let it go at that—quit while you're ahead."

"Oh, yeah," Sammy snapped. "After I finally talk old man Perkins into giving me the reward money, I should just forget about the coin collection? Sure thing. Listen: This dumb town can keep their old weather vane—my partner and I would have had a hard time unloading it anyway. But those coins are something else! There are plenty of collectors who'll be willing to take those coins off my hands with no questions asked." As Sammy spoke, he kept his gun pointed unwaveringly at Miss Lawler.

"But, Sammy, those coins were my responsibility. I—"

"That's the whole point, Cis," Sammy said with a sneer. "When you disappear, everybody's going to assume that you ran off with the coin collection. And the cops will waste all their time looking for you, while me and my sidekick take it easy. I may even stick around Sleepyside for a while and enjoy being a hero."

"Sammy," Miss Lawler said weakly, "you don't mean—"

"What I mean," Sammy interrupted, "is that we're going to take the coins and go for a nice long ride in your big station wagon. And I'm going to come back alone."

"Sammy, please . . ." Miss Lawler pleaded.

"Nobody'll be surprised," Sammy went on. "They know you're an expert on coins. And when they find out about how you flipped out after killing your brother—"

Trixie, hanging on to the top rung of the ladder, covered her mouth with a hand to smother her gasp.

"I didn't! I didn't!" Miss Lawler cried. "It was an accident. You know that."

"Sure, Cis, I know," Sammy crooned. "It was an

accident. You lost control of your car and smashed into a tree. And your poor brother was killed. You flipped out and had to spend some time at a funny farm. Vereee unstable, huh? Just the type to rip off a coin collection and hit the road."

Sammy gestured at the canvas-wrapped bundle. "Get the coins, Cis. I'm going to take you for a long ride."

Trixie was terrified. She had to get help somehow, before Sammy hurt Miss Lawler. Her only hope was to climb back up into the belfry and scream her head off. Maybe someone would hear her and bring help before Sammy could get Miss Lawler out of the building. Trixie pushed on the trapdoor, gently at first, and then harder. It began to open . . . and creaked loudly.

"Who's that?" Sammy demanded. He turned his flashlight upward and spotlighted Trixie, who was cringing against the top rungs of the ladder, pale with terror.

"Well, well," Sammy growled. "It's little Miss Nosy. You must have figured out how I got up on the roof. We were just leaving for a nice long ride . . . and you can come with us. Get down! And you'd better make it fast!"

Trembling with fear, Trixie started down the ladder.

"Come on!" Sammy ordered.

Trixie's foot missed a rung, and she fell with a scream, landing squarely on Sammy. They both crashed to the floor, and Sammy's head hit with a solid *thud*. The gun clattered out of his hand and slid across the room.

At that same moment, the door burst open, and Sergeant Molinson shouted, "Police! Freeze!"

"Boy," Trixie gasped painfully, "am I ever glad to see you!"

Someone else, with a gun in his hand, stepped up behind Sergeant Molinson. It was the bell tower man!

"Look out!" Trixie screamed.

Molinson turned quickly, then relaxed and holstered his gun. "It's okay," he called. "You can all come in now."

Honey and the boys crowded into the room.

"Oh, Trixie!" Honey threw her arms around her friend, unable to say any more.

"Are you all right, Trix?" Brian asked.

"Did he hurt you?" Mart asked.

Trixie's laugh was shaky, and suddenly her knees felt wobbly. She leaned on Honey. "He told me to come down in a hurry," she said. "So I fell on top of him."

Jim wiped his forehead with the back of his hand. "We just got into town, and Honey told us about your little climb," he said. "We got Sergeant Molinson right away."

"You should have come for me sooner, young lady," Sergeant Molinson told Honey gruffly.

Miss Lawler's voice was trembling. "If you hadn't been here, Trixie, I don't know what would have happened."

Trixie smiled weakly and put her arm around the teacher's aide. "Don't think about it," she said. "It's all over now."

Suddenly Trixie's eyes filled with tears, and she hugged Miss Lawler tightly. "I should have known you'd never do anything wrong," she said.

The bell tower man walked over and put a hand on Miss Lawler's shoulder. "I never should have let you stay alone in your apartment," he said. "I figured Sammy was about ready to run again, but I didn't think—"

Miss Lawler smiled. "Trixie's right—it's all over now." Turning to the others, she added, "This is Mr. Gibbons. He's a parole officer from New York."

"I followed Sammy here after he jumped his parole in New York," Mr. Gibbons explained. "He and his partner were released from jail early in the year."

Trixie shook her head. "We—we thought *you* were Sammy's partner," she said.

Mr. Gibbons grinned. "So that's it. This morning in the library, I was going to show you my identification . . . but you ran like scared rabbits."

Sammy groaned and sat up. Sergeant Molinson snapped a pair of handcuffs on him and hauled him to his feet. "Let's go, buster," he said sternly.

As the sergeant led Sammy out of the room, Miss Lawler murmured, "Good-bye, Sammy." There was a moment of uncomfortable silence.

"Somebody better call Moms," Trixie said finally.

"Wait'll she hears about this," Brian said with a sigh.

Mart scratched his head. "Is anybody else besides me hungry?"

"Listen," Honey said cheerfully, "we were going to Wimpy's for dinner. Miss Lawler and Mr. Gibbons, will you join us? We can talk about everything while we eat."

"I have a better idea," Trixie said. "Let's get a takeout order and go back to Crabapple Farm. Then

Moms and Dad can hear about everything, too."

Miss Lawler smiled at the tall parole officer. "I told you the Bob-Whites were wonderful kids," she said.

All talking at once, they headed out the door.

". . . and it was late when we started home," Miss Lawler's soft voice went on with her story. "The storm had been pretty bad, and the roads were icy. I remember my car spinning out of control, and then we hit the tree— When I regained consciousness in the hospital, they told me my brother had been killed."

The Bob-Whites were sprawled on floor cushions, listening while Miss Lawler talked. The adults had moved their chairs close around the blazing fire. Bobby was asleep, his head resting on Reddy's broad back.

"But it wasn't your fault," Trixie whispered.

"I was pretty ill after that," Miss Lawler continued. "I spent some time in a hospital. When I was finally feeling better, I took a job as a counselor in a halfway house."

"Is that where you met Sammy?" Honey inquired sympathetically.

Miss Lawler nodded. "He's the same age my brother was," she said. "I wanted desperately to help him. . . ."

Mr. Gibbons coughed self-consciously. "Sammy had been in jail for theft. Living at the halfway house was one of the conditions of his parole. Sammy is an intelligent young man. He seemed to have a lot of potential, and we all expected him to do well. Then he ran off with his former partner. I tracked them here."

"What about the partner?" Brian asked.

"He was arrested this afternoon," Mr. Gibbons said. "He told me all about the weather vane caper. After that big storm was over, Sammy took advantage of the fact that the streetlights were out. He climbed a tree behind Town Hall, took the weather vane down through the inside of the building, and let himself out the front door. He had arranged for his partner to pick it up on Louis Road the next day, using the song on the radio as a signal. But when Sammy heard about the reward the next day, he changed his plans."

"And he used another song—'St. Louis Blues'—to let his partner know," Trixie concluded.

"Right, Trixie," Mr. Gibbons said.

Miss Lawler shook her head. "Sammy came to me and told me that he knew who had stolen the weather vane and where it was hidden. He begged me to help him return it, and I thought—"

"That's what you were doing when we saw you driving with Sammy in your station wagon!" Honey exclaimed.

"Yes," Miss Lawler said. "I really believed that Sammy wanted to do something good, so I helped him return the weather vane, even though I hadn't been able to make myself drive a car since the accident. I had hired someone to drive my car to Sleepyside when I came. I didn't know that Sammy had stolen the coin collection."

"Well," Mr. Gibbons said, standing, "with all the evidence that you young people collected, Sammy and his partner will be going back to jail for a good long time. You're quite an alert detective, Trixie."

Trixie blushed. "It wasn't too alert of me to think that you were Sammy's partner," she apologized.

"Say, Trixie," Mart began slyly, "perhaps you were in too much haste to baste, after all."

Trixie lifted an eyebrow at him.

"Well," Mart explained, "if you can manage to lose another button from your Bob-White jacket—and I can think of unlikelier occurrences—maybe it will be placed with the other artifacts inside our weather vane before it's recoppered and restored to its perch."

"Gleeps!" Trixie crowed. "I *told* you Hoppy would make us Bob-Whites famous someday!"

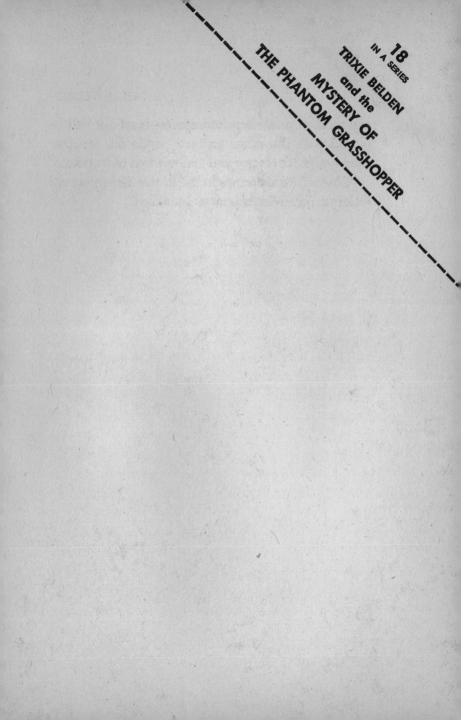